# PLAYING SAFE

This book is intended to provide a basic practical guide to the subject of child safety. It does not pretend to be, nor is it, a comprehensive authority on a far-reaching and complex topic that has significant legal implications.

The aim is to give a useful working knowledge of the subject and simplicity and brevity have taken priority over a wealth of detail. While the book is intended to be an accurate appreciation of the problems, it therefore has its limitations and should be read and understood accordingly.

# PLAYING SAFE

## The parents' guide to children's safety in and out of the home

### SU SAYER

THORSONS PUBLISHING GROUP

First published 1989

*Main illustrations by Jane Redwood
Back cover photograph by Carol Matheson*

British Library Cataloguing in Publication Data

Sayer, Su
Playing safe : the parents' guide to
children's safety in and out of the home.
1. Safety
I. Title
363.1

ISBN 0-7225-1739-4

Prices correct at time of going to press

Published by Thorsons Publishers Limited,
Wellingborough, Northamptonshire NN8 2RQ, England

Printed in Great Britain by Mackays of Chatham, Kent

1   3   5   7   9   10   8   6   4   2

# CONTENTS

# DEDICATION

This book would not have been written without the help of my family — Richard, James and Matthew — who have been my guinea pigs for many years! Two people deserve special thanks — Anne-Marie Love, who has uncomplainingly typed and altered this manuscript scores of times, and my sister, Jane Redwood, who drew many of the illustrations.

# ACKNOWLEDGEMENTS

So many people have helped me both directly and indirectly that space does not permit me to mention them all.

Special thanks, however are due to Nim Barnes of Foresight, Keith Burgin of the British Red Cross Society, Gavin Campbell, Dr Damien Downing, Michele Elliot of Kidscape, Edwin Hooper of RoSPA, Diana Lamplugh of The Suzy Lamplugh Trust, Barry Lonergan, Reebok, Douglas Stewart, The Royal Life-saving Society, Chris Tomlinson of RoSPA, Karen Toole and Debbie Williams also of RoSPA and John Walker of West Sussex Fire Brigade.

# ABOUT THE AUTHOR

Married with two sons, Su Sayer was born in Sussex. She was educated at both a girls' boarding school in Hastings and at a boys' public school near Chichester. At Reading University she graduated with an Honours Degree in Chemical Physics and in 1969 she joined ICI Fibres Division where she worked until 1972.

Su helped found United Response in 1973, a charity that sets up residential homes for people with a handicap. In her work as a Director of the charity, she is closely concerned with the safety of over 300 people — both staff and residents. The charity is committed to encouraging as high a degree of self-reliance as possible whilst supporting residents with enlightened and understanding care. Consequently, residents participate in many of the safety procedures and often contribute to their extension and improvement. In 1987 Su won a RoSPA Award as Safety Officer of the Year. This is an award given to the person who has made the most outstanding contribution to safety in that year.

# FOREWORD

Su Sayer's book *Playing Safe*, provides both a refreshing and practical approach to traditional problems of safety. By combining her experience as a mother and as a safety practitioner she has looked at the lifestyle of the child, a style that the poets remind us should be carefree and happy but which we older and wiser adults know can so easily be marred by injury, disease or death.

In a book that reflects care and common sense, Su Sayer addresses herself to the task of reducing risk — in the home, in the garden, in the playground and (a sad comment but a necessary one) when with other people, for it is only by reducing *risk* that we can increase *safety*. It is by creating greater awareness of hazards that we can take steps to eliminate or control them and thereby make life safer, healthier and happier.

The book is therefore highly recommended reading for all those people who have a responsibility for children, not only parents but also teachers, child-minders, youth workers and community helpers.

E.G. Hooper, OBE
Chief Safety Officer, The Electricity Council
Chairman RoSPA's National Occupational Safety and Health
Committee

# INTRODUCTION

Why a book about safety? Doesn't anyone who has anything to do with children automatically have an inbuilt awareness of the day-to-day hazards in their lives?

The original meaning of hazard was 'a game of dice', but when we talk about safety and safety precautions we are talking about saving lives and this should not be a game of chance. Of course there will always be hazards in all our lives, but in writing this book I am trying to make sure that the dice are heavily loaded . . . in our favour.

The sad truth is that more accidents happen in the home than anywhere else. Although we read of appalling disasters caused by fires, road, air and industrial accidents, terrible as these tragedies are, far more people die or are seriously injured every year in their own home. In 1985 in England and Wales, *40 per cent* of all fatal accidents occurred at home.

I have tried in these 10 chapters to cover many everyday problems that could result in tragedy unless we are all one, if not two or three, steps ahead of the disaster. If we take it seriously we can save untold suffering and misery; if we relax and think it could never happen to us, or that it is someone else's responsibility, we are fools.

Our children rely on us, they trust us and they learn from our example. We must deserve that trust, not by overprotecting, but by thinking ahead, removing the obvious pitfalls and teaching good habits that will last a lifetime. It is a process which is largely self perpetuating — for today's children are the parents of tomorrow.

In this book for 'he' read 'she' and 'she' read 'he'.

# CHAPTER 1

# GENERAL HOUSEHOLD SAFETY

## Harsh facts

- Each year accidents at home in Great Britain account for the deaths of about 5,500 people. A further 3 million seek medical attention following an accident at home.
- Twice as many children require in-patient treatment for home accidents as they do for road accidents. In 1986 776,000 children were taken to hospital as a result of an accident at home. Of these 34,500 were admitted to hospital as in-patients, 26,000 of these were aged under 5.
- The main causes of admission were poisoning, head injuries, burns and fractures.

We could all reduce these statistics dramatically — it's not difficult. *But* to do this we must become much more aware and adopt a far more systematic approach to safety.

The good news about safety and making places safer is that anybody can do it. I can, you can, our children can.

The key to the whole concept of safety is *awareness*. If you and your family can learn what the problems might be and how to avoid them, then you will have fewer accidents. The purpose of this book is to show you how to do this. The aim is to raise your level of awareness, to help you think ahead to anticipate potential accidents and, most importantly, it will show you either how to reduce the risk or avoid it altogether.

Of course, no one is ever going to be perfectly safe. BUT, if any-

thing happens to my family as a
result of an accident, I would like
to feel that I have done my best
and I am sure you feel as I do.
Who could live with themselves
if, just because they hadn't
bothered, their child was badly
hurt?

Anyone concerned with children
has a natural caring instinct —
safety is all about caring for people and as I hope you will agree
when you have read this book, it
really is not difficult.

How often have you walked
around your house, noticed something that looked a little unsafe
and needed attention and
thought 'I must mend that' and
then the telephone has rung or a
little voice has called 'Mummy' or
'Daddy', your attention has been
diverted and you have forgotten
all about the problem? The
answer is 'frequently' — it happens to us all even when our
children are older and are, sup-
posedly, less demanding.

# Safety audits

Safety professionals carry out
very comprehensive safety audits
of their premises: here is a very
simple adaption of that idea
which I have devised and which I
hope will help put your mind at
rest and make your whole family
or household far more safety
conscious.

What is this simple system?
How does it work and can I do it in
my home no matter how big or
small it is?

All you need is enough time to
be able to walk into every room in
your house, and a note pad and
pencil.

## What do I do?
Once a month you should choose

one of the adults in your house to
do a simple safety check. If you
can, rotate the monthly check between the adults in the house
(unless you are the only one!)
because it's amazing how a different pair of eyes can spot different things. I know that when I
do a safety check as part of my job,
I often see things that everyone
else has missed and similarly I
miss things that perhaps the person with me will pick up.

The first couple of times that
you do this safety check it may
take you quite some time,
depending on the size of your
house. Don't worry, once these
initial very thorough checks have
been done and you have

eliminated the major hazards — or have decided that you will have to live with them and have modified the situation in order to reduce the risk — then you will find that safety checks can be done quite quickly and your eye will become trained to pick out any danger or potential danger with comparative ease.

Take your clean notebook and label it *Safety Hazards*. I think it is best to keep a book just for this purpose as then you will have a convenient record of what needs to be done.

Now look around you and see what could cause an accident. Make a list of all the points you notice and what action needs to

Look around and see what could cause an accident

be taken to remedy the problem. As this will probably be the first time that you have ever done a safety check I have made a list of some of the things that you should be looking out for. *These suggestions should not be used as a check list* since there are many other points that *you* will notice. It is very important to keep your mind open and alert to new hazards or safety features rather than relying on a list.

## Living rooms

On average, more accidents (over 20 per cent) to children occur in the living or dining room than in any other part of the house.

## What to look for in your living room

- Is the fireplace adequately and securely guarded?
- Are the lampshades showing any signs of becoming overheated? Are there any brown/burnt patches on the shade of your lamp or has the lampshade slipped (a very common problem) and fallen directly onto the light bulb? Is the correct light bulb being used for the light (e.g., 60 watt, 100 watt, etc.)? Most lampshades and light fittings state the maximum wattage that should be used.
- Are power points that are unused covered with a safety plug? Crawling infants or toddlers love to play with power points and, left to their own devices, would stick metal objects into the holes with great delight. Is the TV unplugged at night?
- Are all electrical appliances turned off at night? Are any of the plugs cracked or showing signs of burning?
- Are any of the wires working loose?
- Are any sockets overloaded with too many plugs?
- Is the carpet or other floor covering safe? Is it slippery or liable to cause someone to trip? (Rugs on highly polished floors can be disastrous.)
- Are all small ornaments positioned safely so that any toddlers cannot reach them?
- Are the door handles loose? A faulty door handle can easily cause a child to be trapped in a room.
- If you have sash windows, are the cords strong and not perished?

- Are your heaters correctly positioned? (Accidents with electric heaters cause 1,300 fires annually.) Keep any heater well away from furniture, curtains, etc. and don't use them to dry clothes.
- Are your waste paper bins made of plastic or wicker? If you have smokers in the house it is far safer to use metal bins in case any discarded cigarette is still smouldering.

Does this give you some idea what to look for? You may find that on the first check you only have time to do one or two rooms but, whenever you get the chance, work through the whole house, writing down the problems you have found.

As you will see I have included lists of hazards for other areas of the house later in the chapter and I hope they will be useful. It is very important, however, that you don't rely solely on these lists. You will see many other hazards as you walk round and you should make a note of these in your book. Use your eyes, ears and nose and a little bit of common sense and I think you will be surprised at what you find.

## Windows

Sometimes I am accused of being over-cautious and over-protective, which may be true, but when you have seen the results of some really appalling accidents I'm afraid it does make you err on the side of caution. I visited the site of an accident where a young lady had fallen out of an upstairs bedroom window and, as a result, is now paraplegic. Look at your upstairs windows and check whether or not they are safe. It is very simple to install a window-locking device that will restrict the aperture of the window. If you do decide that these are necessary, then make sure they are easily and rapidly removeable in the case of fire and explain to your children why the locks are there. Also try to avoid putting furniture directly under windows for children to climb onto.

### Safety glass and film

## Harsh facts

- Approximately 14,000 children in England and Wales seek medical attention at a hospital every year as a result of accidents involving architectural glass.

If you have a French window or glass in some of your doors, or perhaps a low-level window, then there is a risk that your child will run into it, break the glass and cut himself. You can avoid this by using safety glass (BS 6206), which is stronger than ordinary glass. When it does break it is much less likely to cause a serious injury as it doesn't break into large jagged pieces. There are two sorts of safety glass — laminated or toughened.

Laminated glass is made from two sheets of ordinary glass with a sheet of plastic in between. If something crashes into it then the glass is held together by the plastic filling. Toughened glass is specially heated glass and when it breaks it shatters into small, rounded pieces. If a bedroom window is low, safety glass is a must to prevent anyone falling through.

Another way of protecting your child from large areas of glass is to cover the glass with a safety film (obtainable from Mothercare.) This is a clear plastic film that is spread onto one surface of the glass and it holds the glass together if it gets broken. It is much cheaper than safety glass and, provided it is correctly fitted, can be very effective. Make sure you follow the manufacturer's instructions carefully.

# Glass-topped coffee tables

Many of these are made from ordinary plate glass rather than the toughened variety. Think about a child climbing onto your coffee table. The glass is held firm by the outer casing — often stainless steel. Use your imagination: the glass breaks, the edges remain rigid and the jagged fragments tear into your child's legs as he falls. With safety glass, this would be prevented.

Remember too, that glass-topped tables that are not edged with metal or cane are difficult to see. That glass edge can be lethal.

Unfortunately there is no legal obligation for manufacturers to use safety glass — but the price you pay may be a child who is scarred for life.

# The nursery

The most common cause of death in children over one year old is an accident.

One would think that if a baby hadn't reached the crawling stage there wouldn't be many hazards in a nursery. How I wish this were true! Let's look at some of the ways these accidents can happen.

Just consider what is in a nor-

# What to look for in your bedrooms

- Are any suitcases or other items stored on top of cupboards or wardrobes likely to fall down and cause an accident?
- Have you a mirror that might reflect the sunlight on to a curtain or other flammable surface? I have seen a curtain and a wooden table badly scorched from this — one of them was in my house! Be particularly careful of magnifying 'vanity' mirrors.
- Check electrical plugs.
- Check lampshades — never cover them to reduce glare.
- Check for loose door handles.
- Check flooring.
- Is the exit route from the bed to the door clear at night? Make sure that there are no toys or model train sets, lego, etc. on the floor to cause a child to fall, either whilst on a night-time expedition to the bathroom or in the (hopefully) unlikely event of a fire. It is important that there is a clear, straightforward, uncluttered exit route.
- Are all wardrobes and chests of drawers secure so that if a child swings on a door or a drawer handle the piece of furniture will not topple over on to him? (I'm afraid this happens all too often.)
- Check for sharp edges.
- Check for medicines in your bedside cabinet. They should be locked up.
- Make sure no lights or table lamps are too close to any curtains, clothing or bedding. It is easy to start a fire this way.

mal nursery: a cot — containing a cot mattress, a cot sheet and some form of covering to keep the baby warm; there will probably be a changing mat, possibly a play mat, perhaps a high chair for use when the baby can sit up, a cot bumper and a variety of cuddly toys. How many of these items are filled with polyurethane foam? As of February 1989 new furniture and mattresses must be made to much higher standards, but until all the old foam-filled items are thrown away, nurseries will be high-risk areas.

## What should you be aiming for?

Try to make sure that all bedding is flame retardant and has passed the flammability test BS 5438. The cot should comply with BS 1753 and the cot mattress with BS 1877. *Never never* smoke in your baby's nursery. Quite apart from the risks of passive smoking, it is so easy to put a cigarette down and for the telephone to ring and for disaster to strike whilst you're out of the room.

Make sure that all the toys meet the flammability requirement of BS 5665 and, if you're not sure, then check your furry friend in the way that I have described on page 60.

### Cellular blankets
Whilst these can be wonderfully warm and light, they can cause problems for babies and small children. Toes and fingers can get caught in the weave and loose threads can become wound round them and cause an injury. It is safest not to use them.

### Cot bumpers
These are often secured to the cot by ties. If these are too long they can get caught round a baby's limbs — or worse still round his neck. Make sure the ties are as short as is practicable.

### Suffocation
Certainly no baby under two should have a pillow because of the danger from suffocation. Also, be very careful about any plastic items or plastic coverings that have previously wrapped an article. Some of the flimsy plastic is particularly dangerous and can not only smother a child but can also get in a child's throat and may well block his airway. Take it off cot mattresses, etc. before you ever use them and tear up and throw away any plastic bags. If you want to reuse them, store them well away from any small children. If your child uses one of the stiff, plastic bibs, take it off as soon as the meal is over and keep plastic pants out of the way.

### Baby walkers
I'm afraid I am very unhappy about the use of baby walkers. A child who uses one *must be watched constantly if you are to avoid an accident.*

The walker can tip and over-balance, it may crash into doors, tables, etc. and the child may be badly hurt. In one survey that was done the injuries included:

- burns
- scalds (the children were able to reach a hot drink on a hot surface because they were in a walker)
- cuts and lacerations (mainly to the face and head).

Many of the accidents in the survey showed that the adult who was supervising had either just moved out of view and the child was trying to move towards the adult or was busy doing something else when disaster struck. The BS number for baby walkers is 4648. It has recently been upgraded to try and eliminate some of these accidents but the message is clear: *never ever leave a child on his own in a baby walker — it is just not safe.*

## Second-hand equipment

Baby equipment is frequently passed from person to person. My pram, cot and pushchair have all been used by both my sister's children, which means that they are now at least 10 years old. It is essential to check second-hand equipment very thoroughly. There may be new British Standards (the item may be filled with substandard polyurethane foam) or it may quite simply be too old to be safe. Be especially careful of second-hand toys as the standards for toys have recently been revised and many comply to the old British Standard number. The old British Standard number is BS 3443; the new one is BS 5665.

## Bathrooms

Recently I had to investigate a situation where someone had been severely scalded in a bath.

Even though that person had only been in contact with the hot water for less than a minute he had extensive burns and there was a possibility that he might need a skin graft. This was an adult; a child's skin is much more vulnerable to excesses of temperature and even a very short exposure to water that is too hot can cause the most appalling burns.

It only takes five seconds to cause a severe burn from water of 60°C(150°F.) Check your domestic hot water and make sure that you have a thermostat that adequately regulates it. Often the thermostat is set unnecessarily high — turn it down to the lowest setting that is practicable (I have mine at 50°C/ 132°F). At bath-time teach your child to run the cold tap first and to add the hot water later. Make sure you always test the water before your child gets in and teach him to do the same. The good news is that there are some excellent valves that will thermostatically control the temperature of your water at the tap and these are well worth fitting. One manufacturer is Caradon Mira (see page 164 for their address). Ask a plumber about these now.

Don't leave a young child in the bath on his own, it is all too easy for him to drown. Teach him never to play with the taps.

Radiators too can easily burn, especially in the bathroom when the child has no clothes on to protect him. Turn the radiator down to a safe level.

*Showers and hand showers* should be thermostatically controlled and have a fail-safe device that ensures the temperature is always regulated. Imagine what would happen if the cold water supply was interrupted for some reason . . . the hot water would continue to flow — with disastrous consequences for the bather. Check your hot water and showers now and prevent some of the terrible scalding accidents that happen every year (the Mira valve can be used here too).

### Gas water heaters and gas appliances

Any gas appliance that malfunctions can cause death from carbon monoxide poisoning. Make sure yours are regularly serviced and used correctly.

Gas water heaters should be of the balanced flue variety. Check that the outside vent is kept clear — dead birds or leaves can clog it up. All too often the would-be bather shivering from the draught, decides to block off the air vent in the bathroom. Result: a build-up of deadly carbon monoxide fumes.

## What to look for in your bathroom

- Are your loo cleaners (cleaning fluids, bleach or equivalent) well out of reach of small children?
- Is your carpet or floor covering safe?
- Check your lampshades and light fittings
- Check your door handles
- Is the handbasin loose?
- Check for sharp edges, particularly around any vanity units.

## What to look for in your loft

This is an area that is often neglected. It may not need checking every month after the first initial and very thorough check, but, nevertheless, it should be checked on a regular basis and you should decide for yourself how often you are going to check it and you should stick to this.

One of the greatest risks in a loft is that of fire. If you are like me your loft will be crammed full of suitcases, papers and toys, Christmas decorations and clothes I wish I hadn't bought.

Is there any likelihood that the light in your loft can be left on and a fire could start? Flammable items stored or stacked too near a hot light bulb can easily start a fire.

Notice if there are any leaks in the roof. Could water accumulate on the loft floor and cause the ceiling below to collapse?

Is the ladder leading to the loft safe, properly installed and stored well away from interested small boys and girls? Beware of cracks in the wood.

## What to look for in your cellar

Are you lucky enough to have a cellar? Oh, to be able to banish to a cellar the Spanish plonk that clutters up my kitchen after a family holiday! Make sure, however that:

- flammable items (methylated spirits, turpentine, etc.) are stored upright, with the lids well on and away from any heat source, hot pipes, etc.
- check lampshades (do you really need one in the cellar? A bare bulb may be much safer)
- check sockets and plugs.

Check that there is adequate lighting both at the top and bottom of the staircase leading into your cellar and make sure that there is a switch at the top of the steps rather than just at the bottom.

Make sure too that the cellar steps are not slippery and not too narrow and steep. I remember reading with horror how David Niven's first wife fell down some cellar steps and was killed — be very careful and make sure that you can lock your cellar door and remove the key so that small children are not at risk.

## Falls

### Harsh facts

- In 1986 an estimated 22,000 children under five fell from stairs and were taken to hospital.
- Another survey showed that 11 per cent of falls for babies under one year old occurred while the baby was being held by another person who either fell himself or dropped the baby. In over half these cases that person was the child's mother.
- In the same survey in 44 per cent of all falls (for babies under one year old) the baby fell off a raised level — prams, baby-walkers, high, low and bouncing chairs and beds were all culprits.

Babies are much more mobile than we think. Don't leave them alone unless you are absolutely

sure they cannot fall or injure themselves.

## Stairs and banisters

Make sure your stair carpet is not loose. It could cause someone to trip. Check also that your banisters are secure and not wobbly.

Please, please remember always to carry your baby so that you have one hand free to grab the banister if you trip. It is all too tempting to use that other hand to carry a bag of dirty washing or something. Don't! Play safe and keep one hand free.

*Balconies* can be very danger-ous for young children. Horizon-tal balcony railings are parti-cularly dangerous because they are so easy to climb. Board them up or fit wire netting guards and keep the door to any balcony loc-ked so that your child can't ven-ture out alone.

## The kitchen

There are so many things to be aware of in a kitchen that the next chapter will deal entirely with the problems that arise and how to make your kitchen safer. You will then have a good idea of what you should be looking for and how to avoid many of the hazards.

## What to look for in your garage or garden shed

Garages tend to become a refuge for all the things you don't want in the house, but can't bear to give away. All too often lawn mowers, petrol cans and paint pots nestle dangerously near bags of jumble and outgrown children's clothes. Tools should be locked away in a tool kit box so that no child will be tempted to try a little woodwork when you're not around.

Children love to copy adults and I remember how alarmed I was when I found my small son, then aged three, attempting to copy his father. He was standing by our lawnmower, pulling the starter motor string and repeating the magic words that Daddy always uses when he starts the machine '... Oh damn, Oh damn'!

I learned three major lessons from that incident:
- if you don't want your children to use bad language don't use it yourself!
- make sure that items are pro-perly stored away and that the door to your garage or shed is kept well secured.
- make sure any power tool is left disconnected. Remove the sparkplug if necessary.

# Rectifying the situation

Right, so by now you've done your safety audit, you've walked all round your house and you've listed all the points that could cause an accident.

## What should I do now?

There are four ways to cope with the risks that you have found and in the safety world they are known as the 'four t's.'

- treat
- terminate
- tolerate
- transfer

You must now decide which of the four t's you are going to employ.

## Treat

This means dealing with the problem directly. For example, if the handle of your frying pan is wobbly, take a screwdriver and tighten the screw. The problem should then be solved and you could put a tick by that item on your list of hazards.

## Terminate

This means getting rid of the problem so that it cannot happen again. Let's say you found an old rusty nail sticking out of the wall.

You would terminate that risk by pulling it out of the wall. The problem is then solved and will not reappear (at least not unless you have a phantom nail inserter somewhere in your house!)

## Tolerate

This means that you would consider the risk and, for various reasons, decide to tolerate it. For example, let's take the case of kitchen cupboards with sharp edges. You may, like me, have inherited these and the thought of changing all those doors is enough to make your bank balance go red in anticipation. There is probably little you can do to treat this problem and the only other method of eliminating the risk would be to terminate it by changing the cupboard doors, which we have already decided is far too costly. So, you may decide to live with this. Try to think of one or two things that could reduce the risk and perhaps you will able to implement these.

What I did was to make sure that everyone knew of the dangers and kept the cupboard doors closed. Then I tried to keep my children, when they were little, in a part of the kitchen where there were no cupboards or in a high chair or playpen out of harm's way while I was cooking.

Apply your mind to each problem and ask yourself 'Can I terminate it or must I live with it?' *It is for you to decide.*

## Transfer

The final method of coping with the risk is to transfer the risk to someone else and, in this case, it would probably be your insurance company. Clearly there are some eventualities that, despite all your care, may *still* happen. For example, you may still have a fire in your house. Most people would prefer to insure themselves against this sort of damage.

You may now be reeling at the thought of doing a safety check in your own house. However, the first one is always the worst and thereafter you will find that they become quicker and easier and soon you are able to do them simply in the time that it takes to walk around your house. I do them with my children and we make a game of it: each one of us scores a point for every hazard that we see and the person that has scored the most points at the end gets a prize.

I also use this system at work in our homes for people with a mental handicap and the results have been excellent. Not only have we raised the general safety standard dramatically, but we have also made everyone very aware of the importance of safety and of how easily accidents can happen. The result has *not* been to make people worry — quite the reverse, everyone has enjoyed the involvement and they are very proud of their homes.

# Electrical safety

Some 25,000 fires in homes each year are caused by electrical faults or by people misusing electrical equipment. Over 2,000 people are killed or injured as a result. Teach your children to treat electricity with respect.

There are some simple electrical jobs that can be done without professional help — others cannot. Play safe — if in any doubt at all contact your local Electricity Board or a qualified electrician. Have your wiring installation checked regularly.

## Remember:

- don't overload circuits
- avoid using multi-way adaptors. One appliance, one socket, is safest
- use purpose-made extension leads if extra cord length is needed
- make sure that extension leads are completely uncoiled from their drums before use. They get very hot otherwise and could cause a fire
- always make sure your hands are dry when you operate anything electrical
- unplug leads with care: hold and pull on the plug, not the lead.

## Electric blankets

There are 1,800 electric blanket fires each year resulting in about 35 deaths. More than half of these fires are due to faults. Check that your blanket conforms to BS 3456, make sure it is stored dry and flat and is serviced at least every two or three years. Follow the manufacturer's instructions carefully.

In one trial in Warwickshire 8,000 electric underblankets were collected from people's homes and tested — of these nearly 75 per cent needed replacing or servicing!

# Checking your electrical equipment

The bad news is that this can be time-consuming: the good news is that, after the first major check, you really only need to do this thorough check every six months. Bear with me, this is probably one of the most important checks that you will ever do. Remember that, on average, faults in wiring cause over 2,000 fires every year.

## What do I need?

Arm yourself with a couple of screwdrivers for unscrewing plugs, a packet of 3 amp and 13 amp fuses, a wire stripper and your notebook.

## When should I do it?

It's best to do this either in the evening or when the children are out of the house.

## How do I do it?

You are going to check that each electrical item is properly wired to its plug, and that it has the correct fuse.

To do this, first examine the plug externally. Is it cracked? In which case, discard and replace it. Is it hot or discoloured from overheating? If so check that the correct fuse is being used (see the Notes on page 35) and that the plug is properly wired. If none of these appears to be causing the problem DO NOT USE that particular piece of equipment. Either remove it or take the plug off so that it can't be used and if there are other people staying in the house (visitors, lodgers, etc.) put a notice on it saying that 'This item is dangerous – DO NOT USE.' You should then get that piece of equipment checked by a competent electrician.

Do the wires feel loose? Open the plug, look at the wiring. Is it correctly wired (see diagram of a correctly wired plug below)? Are

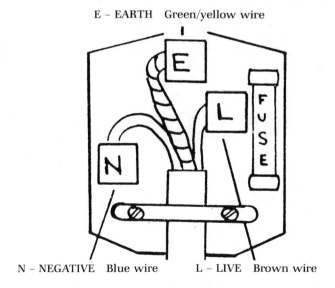

E – EARTH   Green/yellow wire

N – NEGATIVE   Blue wire          L – LIVE   Brown wire

How to wire a plug correctly

all the leads secure? Is the correct fuse being used? If everything looks fine, you can then screw back the cover and go on to the next plug.

This does sound a little time consuming, but if you could see the number of times I find that one of the wires has worked its way loose and is wandering around the plug or that a plug is actually wrongly wired or that the inside of the plug is beginning to burn, you wouldn't begrudge spending a little time to get it right.

## Residual current circuit breakers

Have you read the horrific stories in the newspapers about people electrocuting themselves when they have severed the electric lead to their hedge clippers or lawn mower? We all need protection from this kind of disaster, not only in the garden but also in the home, and one of the best ways of avoiding an electrical accident is to install residual current circuit breakers in your fuse box. These are devices that cut off the current (by breaking the circuit) should there be any current leakage.

As a result of publicity by Esther Rantzen on the 'That's Life' television programme a number of households have now fitted these RCCBs in their fuseboxes. Consult an electrician and discuss the installation of these — they can usually be fitted very easily and quickly, are not very expensive and in my view are worth every penny.

You can also use individual power breakers (obtainable from hardware and DIY shops) that contain RCCBs for individual electrical items. These are especially good for using with outdoor power tools if RCCBS have not yet been fitted in the fuse box. Look for BS 1363 and 4293.

## Fuse boxes and mains

These should be simply labelled showing which fuse is for which area. Also, keep a list showing exactly where all the power sources can be turned off. For example:

- gas mains — large switch in garage near meter
- water mains — tap under sink — turn to the left until tight
- hot water supply — red wheel in airing cupboard by middle shelf — turn to the right.

Check these simple facts and make sure everyone has access to them so that you will be prepared in an emergency.

Our children spend a major part of their childhood in their own home. We owe it to them to try and make home a safe environment in which to live and play and it is well worth spending a little time to achieve this. Start checking one room at a time and you will see just how many risks you are taking at the moment and how very easy it is to make your house a much much safer place.

## Notes on the correct use of fuses

A suspect fuse, not bearing the BSI Kitemark. NOT RECOMMENDED

A creditable fuse displays BSI Kitemark and ASTA Diamond. RECOMMENDED

*ASTA — The Association of Short Circuit Testing Authority

BSI Kitemark — British Standards Institution
BS 1362: 1973 — General purpose fuse links for domestic and similar purposes

- Use a 3 amp fuse for appliances up to 720 watts. Always check the manufacturer's instructions but normally you will use 3 amp fuses for appliances such as:
  radios          food mixers
  tablelamps      hedgecutters
  liquidizers     strimmers

- Use a 13 amp fuse for appliances rated over 720 watts. However, there are also some appliances with motors — such as vacuum cleaners and spin dryers that should also have 13 amp fuses. *Always check the manufacturer's instructions.* 13 amp fuses are usually used for appliances such as:

kettles
refrigerators
electric fires
toasters
washing machines
tumble dryers
dishwashers
lawnmowers

Fuses should bear the BSI Kitemark as well as the British Standard Number, which, for fuses is BS 1362.

Some fuses will also bear the ASTA Diamond (see the diagram on page 35.) ASTA is the Association of Short Circuit Testing Authority. In 1982 over 20 million fuses were imported into the UK from the Far East. Samples of these fuses were tested by ASTA and found to be drastically sub-standard. Many fuses being used today bear only a trade name and the BS 1362 number. Tests have proved that such fuses do not comply with BS 1362. Use of these fuses represents a serious fire risk and they should be replaced; so make sure you only buy fuses bearing the BSI Kitemark.

So, good luck with your safety checks. Don't try to do them all at once, just tackle one room at a time and you'll be surprised how good you become at identifying trouble spots *before* rather than *after* the event.

# CHAPTER 2

# SAFETY IN THE KITCHEN

## Harsh facts

- In 1986 62,000 children (aged under 15) were seriously injured in the kitchen. Of these 42,000 were aged under five.

How lovely it would be to start again in a brand new kitchen that you could design for yourself and eliminate all the problems you have ever encountered. However, I don't think that there is such a thing as a perfect kitchen and I'm certain that there is no such thing as a perfectly safe kitchen. People are their own built-in safety hazard — no matter how many safety features *you* 'build in' they must still be used correctly and even a kitchen that is, on the face of it, a safety officer's dream becomes a high-risk area with spilt fat on the floor and an over-full chip pan on the cooker.

The good news is that any kitchen can be made safer by YOU.

So — in an ideal world, how would we design our kitchen? First, *there should be no sharp edges*. Work surfaces should be rounded and have curved corners and cupboard doors should be smooth edged and not have nasty stainless steel corners that are sharp and jut out. A small child could easily fall and cut his face.

Second, the *design* of the kitchen should be such that there is some space where your child can play safely away from the general cooking area. You will then be able to chat to him whilst you cook and he won't feel left out. If the kitchen really is too small for that, then you will need a good highchair that he can sit in (safely harnessed depending on his age) and then he can play, perhaps with some dough or a couple of wooden spoons and a small baking tray, while you cook.

# Storage

What are some of the potentially dangerous things we have in our kitchens?
- knives
- scissors
- forks
- glasses
- matches
- heavy cast iron dishes
- glass dishes
- bleach and other chemicals
- medicines
- oven cleaner and other cleaning agents
- aerosols

'Help', I can hear you saying — 'I haven't enough high cupboards to put all of those in!'

Let's work through the list.

## Knives and scissors

---

### Harsh facts

- In 1986 there were 26,000 accidents involving domestic knives — 39,000 if you include carving knives as well!

---

Keep your kitchen knives and scissors and any other large cutlery items that could cut or poke into a child's eye on a magnetic rack or on hooks out of your child's reach.

Remember, for your own safety, never to leave sharp knives in a sink full of soapy water. It's so easy to be distracted and then come back to the washing up and give yourself quite a nasty cut as you fish through the soap suds trying to discover what you've left in there.

Other small cutlery items should be placed in a drawer that is fitted with a safety stop to prevent the drawer from being pulled out completely. You can buy these in most hardware shops and certainly in many of the major high street chemists.

Teach your children always to carry scissors with the point downwards — and to walk, not run. Small children should use their own special round ended scissors.

## Glasses

Store your glasses (unless they really are unbreakable) in a cupboard above worktop level.

## Cast iron dishes

These are very heavy and I certainly wouldn't like *my* foot to be underneath if I dropped one of these; a child could be badly hurt if one of them fell on him. They are best stored near the floor where they have less distance to fall. It may be a good idea to put a safety catch on the cupboard door.

## Glass dishes

In the wrong hands these can break. So, store them either out of harm's way or in a cupboard with a safety catch until your child is old enough to understand the dangers.

## Medicines

These should always be stored in a locked cabinet and *not*, unless there is a VERY GOOD REASON in a fridge. (See the chapter on First Aid, page 102, for more facts.)

## Chemicals

These cause some very serious accidents so I'm going to write about these in more detail.

Some of the chemicals you have in your kitchen may include:

- bleach
- caustic soda
- disinfectant
- fire lighter
- glue
- insecticide
- mothballs
- oven cleaner
- paint
- methylated spirits
- turpentine
- shoe polish
- paraffin
- ammonia
- air freshener
- dry cleaning fluid
- garden chemicals
- aerosols
- fly sprays

Most people store these items under the sink. If you do, then make absolutely sure *there is no way* that your small child can get inside the cupboard.

When he is old enough to understand, then you will be able to show him how dangerous these items are. Even the smell of bleach is pretty offensive, and so is oven cleaner. My boys were quick to realize that these items were real 'no, no's' and they certainly didn't want to go anywhere near them. Until you are quite sure that your children understand the dangers then you *must*

keep these items in an inaccess-
ible place.

The following very basic rules
apply when handling chemicals
generally and I think it's very
important to stick to them if you
are to avoid what could be a very
nasty accident either to yourself
or your family.

## Basic rules for handling household chemicals

• Store chemicals in a safe place,
  either away from children or in
  a cupboard with a safety lock.
  Don't place them on a very
  high shelf as they may spill as
  you lift them off the shelf and
  you may get bleach, etc. on your
  clothing or, worse still, in your
  eye.
• NEVER decant chemicals from
  their original container into
  another for storage. It is very
  important that anyone (for
  example a visitor to your house)
  can see immediately from the
  container what it contains and
  what the manufacturer's recommendations are.
• Always read the label before
  use and follow the instructions carefully.
• Avoid ingestion, inhalation and
  skin contact with all chemical
  substances.
• Wear rubber gloves and an
  apron if you think you might get
  some of the chemical on you. Be

very careful about anything
splashing near your eye.
• NEVER MIX PRODUCTS – you
  could cause a chemical reaction. For example, bleach will
  give off chlorine gas if mixed
  with an acid cleanser such as
  Harpic. So, before you sprinkle
  Harpic down your loo make
  sure that no one else has left
  some bleach in the pan.

Opposite are some of the symbols
that are being used on chemicals
that you should look out for.

Chemical agent monitors are
machines, designed to measure
the concentration of nerve gas
vapour in the atmosphere and are
used by the Army to alert them to
the dangers of chemicals used in
warfare. However Army chemical
warfare instructors, using these
monitors in more peaceful surroundings, have discovered that
they obtain high readings when
nerve agent based fly sprays have
been used. *Myosis, the early
symptom of nerve gas poisoning,
is characterized by dilation of the
pupils* (and at this stage the Army
would begin to treat casualties.)
*Yet, chemical warfare instructors
have found sufficient toxicity to
produce myosis in children of
three and under, from nerve
agent-based fly sprays.* The brain
is still developing in babies and

Toxic

Irritant

Explosive

Flammable

Corrosive

**Warning symbols: all warning symbols are in black on a yellow background**

Harmful

Oxidizing

**Dangerous substances: all dangerous substances symbols are in black on an orange background**

small children so they are much more vulnerable to nerve gases.

Since we can't all have chemical agent monitors set up in our homes to alert us to the concentrations of nerve gases perhaps we should all invest in good old-fashioned fly swats rather than endanger our babies, children and pets by using any nerve agent-based insecticides.

# The cooker

Whether you have an upright cooker, a separate hob or an oven with the hob above it, there are several things you can do to prevent your child being scalded or burnt, either from touching the hot plates or burners or from pulling the pan off the top of the cooker onto himself.

• Buy a cooker guard. Most branches of Mothercare and many hardware shops stock these. They are usually designed so that they will fit onto most cookers or hobs and make it difficult for anything to be pulled off or for little fingers to reach the hot plates or gas burners.
• Train everyone who uses the kitchen to *turn the pan handles inwards* so that there is nothing for a child to clutch. *Use the back rings whenever possible.*
• Saucepan and frying pan handles can easily work loose. Check that there are no screws that need tightening.
• If you have a gas cooker is the pilot light on?
• Cooker hoods and extractor fans: these can easily become clogged with fat deposits and create quite a fire hazard. They should be cleaned regularly.

# Electrical items

## Kettles

Avoid letting the leads of any electrical items dangle over the top of the work surface. Things like this are very tempting to a toddler. Every year hundreds of children are severely scalded — and scarred for life — many from accidents with kettles. Push your

Beware of trailing electric leads

kettle to the back of the work sur-face and *never* let its lead trail over the edge. Wherever possible use a coiled flex.

## Irons

Hot irons are a real hazard. Where possible use a flex holder to pre-vent the flex from trailing and NEVER EVER leave an iron (hot or cold) on the ironing board when you are out of the room. The point-ed tip of the iron could be fatal if it fell on the soft skull of a baby.

# Food and hygiene

I apologize if some of this seems to be stating the obvious but, it is a subject I am constantly being asked for advice on, particularly with the fear of contamination from infectious diseases.

## Some basic rules for good hygiene in the kitchen

- Always wash your hands before handling food.
- Keep any cuts covered with a waterproof dressing.
- Always use a separate knife to cut raw meat. Raw meat contains a number of harmful bacteria that can easily contaminate other foods and cause food poisoning.
- Always scrub your chopping board between using it for different types of foods and if possible use a separate chopping board for raw meat.
- Always wash your hands before and after handling raw meats or fish and before touching cooked meat.
- Keep anywhere that food is prepared spotlessly clean.
- Store raw food and cooked food on different shelves in the refrigerator with the raw food in a place where it won't drip on to anything else. Check that the refrigerator door closes properly. Faulty door seals can let the temperature inside rise and allow bacteria to thrive!
- Always defrost foods thoroughly before cooking or serving. (*Never refreeze food that has been defrosted.*)
- Never smoke whilst you are handling food (ash may drop on to it and there is a risk of transmitting germs from your mouth via your hands).
- Ensure that chicken, turkey, sausages, etc. are cooked through thoroughly. Micro-organisms such as salmonella need to be killed by cooking and you must ensure that the heat reaches all the way through the food so that none of these harmful bacteria can survive.

# Other areas that could spell disaster

## Things that pinch

Look out for things that can pinch fingers. Ironing boards and doors are two of the worst offenders. Doors are particularly lethal at the hinge side. Swing doors cause small children quite a problem since they cannot time their exit with a swing and they often end up trapped on one side or else squashed between the two doors. Sliding doors too can cause problems.

## Freezers

Be very careful about anything that a child can get into but not out of. Chest freezers make a particularly deadly hiding place. Watch too that the hinge mechanisms on your freezer lid are fully functional and that the lid will stay open of its own accord without you having to hold it with one hand whilst reaching in to find that elusive frozen chicken.

Make sure your children understand *why* things like freezers are out of bounds.

## Ovens

Oven doors can get very hot. Some are much better than others so try and check this out when you buy yours. If you're stuck with what you've got and it's one of the badly designed ovens, be aware, and make your children aware too.

When was your microwave oven last checked for microwave leakage? Follow your manufacturer's recommendations.

# Floors

Remember, wearing socks without shoes makes your shiny kitchen floor into a skating rink. It's much better to let your children go barefoot if they don't want to wear shoes.

Vinyl flooring can sometimes crack or turn up at the edges making it easy for someone to trip and fall — perhaps whilst carrying a hot casserole dish. It could prove disastrous, not only to your casserole but also for the small child nearby. Wipe up spills immediately — they can make a floor very slippery.

# Eating in the kitchen

I think if I had a choice I would always eat in the kitchen. The atmosphere is warm and relaxed, it is the focal point of the household, no one ever stands on ceremony and it is the place where wonderful Sunday morning breakfasts are had — with a seemingly endless procession of hot rolls, scrambled eggs and bacon and a coffee pot that seems bottomless.

Often it is when we are most relaxed and not concentrating that an accident can happen.

Beware of oven-to-table pots, which can be very hot and will hold the heat for some time.

Watch out for spilling coffee or tea over your child. Many a child still bears the scars of such a burn. Never leave cups of tea or coffee anywhere near small children and never drink your tea or coffee with a child in your arms. Children are notorious wrigglers — and both of you will be at risk from your hot drink.

*Note*: Approximately 5 per cent of home accidents to children under five are caused by hot drinks.

Never leave cups of hot drink anywhere near small children

# The biscuit tin

Where do you keep your biscuit tin? Out of reach so that little hands can't rifle it? Don't tempt fate. Sooner or later your child will climb up and try to reach it. The weight of the tin may unbalance him and he will fall. Leave the biscuit tin somewhere within reach and teach your children to ask before they help themselves.

# Tablecloths

It really is better not to use a tablecloth when you have small children around. If you must, then remember it is all too easy for a small child to pull on the tablecloth and end up with everyone's meal on his head!

With that happy thought let's move on to think about fire.

# CHAPTER 3

# FIRE

Safety is not something that is best left to the experts — all of us can make our homes safer. Most of these fires could have been avoided — with just a little thought.

## What causes a fire?

As all good boy scouts know, if you want to have a fire you need three ingredients.

**The triangle of combustion**
The three components of a fire are heat, fuel and oxygen. When they are combined in sufficient quantity, a fire will start.

Heat

If you exclude any one of these elements, even if the other two are present, you cannot have a fire. For example, if you remove the fuel from the fire it will burn itself out; if you remove the heat by pouring on cold water, that will extinguish the fire; remove the oxygen by suffocating the fire with, say, a fire blanket or with foam and it will be unable to burn.

Below is a brief summary of what is available generally to help you fight fires.

# Fire extinguishers

Whatever type or make of fire extinguisher you choose, make sure it conforms to the appropriate British Standard. BS 5423 is the Standard for portable fire extinguishers; BS 6165 is for the cheaper small, low-powered extinguishers of the aerosol type. If it carries the BSI Kitemark or has the special BAFE mark (British Approvals for Fire Equip-ment) you will know that the product has been independently tested for safety.

You can get details of approved products and advice on where to obtain them from British Approvals for Fire Equipment (see Useful Addresses, page 163). They can also supply a list of companies approved to service portable fire extinguishers.

Extinguishers can be red with a coloured insert panel or band to indicate the contents:
- blue for dry powder
- black for carbon dioxide
- cream for foam
- green for BCF (Halon)
- red for water.

Others are completely blue, black, cream, etc. Others are self-coloured metal with a coloured insert or band.

Kitemark

BAFE Mark

# Fire extinguisher colour coding

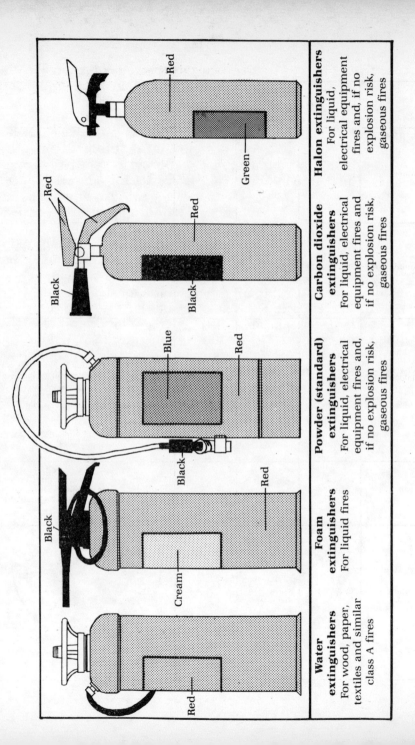

**Water extinguishers**
For wood, paper, textiles and similar class A fires

**Foam extinguishers**
For liquid fires

**Powder (standard) extinguishers**
For liquid, electrical equipment fires and, if no explosion risk, gaseous fires

**Carbon dioxide extinguishers**
For liquid, electrical equipment fires and, if no explosion risk, gaseous fires

**Halon extinguishers**
For liquid, electrical equipment fires and, if no explosion risk, gaseous fires

## Fire Extinguishers

| Type | Colour | Type A (Solids, paper, wood, fabrics etc.) | Type B (liquids, fats, paints, petrol etc.) | Comments |
|------|--------|--------------------------------------------|---------------------------------------------|----------|
| Water | Red | ✓ | X | Heavy and cumbersome (minimum recommended size 5 litres/8.8 pints). Since you often have no idea of what is causing the fire, if possible avoid these.<br><br>DO NOT USE ON ELECTRICAL APPLIANCES |
| Multipurpose Dry Powder | Blue | ✓ | ✓ | Portable, not intrusive (minimum recommended size 1 kg/2 · 2 lb). Powder is messy and if used on delicate electrical equipment (e.g., a home computer), it may well damage it. In general, however, the most practical for domestic situations. |
| Halon (BCF) | Green | ✓ | ✓ | Especially good for fires involving liquids. No mess, portable (minimum recommended size 1.5 kg/3.3 lbs). Good for use on live electrical equipment and an excellent choice for use in cars.<br>**Caution**: the fire may well flare up again as this extinguisher doesn't cool the fire well and also the fumes in an enclosed space can be harmful. |
| Foam | Cream | ✓ | ✓ | Works by squirting foam over the fire and excluding the oxygen. Minimum recommended size 1.5 litres/2½ pints. Best for liquid fires but **not** for chip pans. |
| Carbon Dioxide $CO_2$ | Black | X (Not very effective) | ✓ | Excellent for use on live electrical equipment – it will not damage it. Works by excluding the oxygen. Only effective where fires are limited to a small area.<br>**Caution**: the $CO_2$ is very cold when released and will often cause ice to form round the exit funnel – DO NOT HOLD THIS FUNNEL, your finger may freeze temporarily to it.<br>When you press the trigger, it makes a very loud noise! Don't drop it in fright. |

Please remember: NEVER USE ANY TYPE OF EXTINGUISHER ON A CHIP PAN OR FAT FIRE. The force of the jet may splash the fat out of the pan and it is much safer to use a fire blanket.

There are two main types of fire:
- type A — caused by solid materials, e.g., paper, wood, cloth, plastic etc.
- type B — caused by liquids, fats, oils, paints, petrol, etc.

Do remember that, whichever extinguishers you choose, you should have them serviced regularly (once a year is usually enough.) Keep them well away from small children who may be tempted to play with them. Check them yourself to make sure they don't feel lighter than usual (which may indicate someone has used them!) or that the safety plug hasn't been removed.

# Fire blankets

Even if you decide not to have any fire extinguishers a fire blanket is an absolute MUST for any kitchen. It is safest, in a domestic situation never to use any extinguisher on a chip pan or fat fire. SO FOR A FAT FIRE (chip pans, frying pans, grill pans, etc.) USE A FIRE BLANKET. By using a fire blanket correctly you can save your family from a major disaster. Any fire blanket (minimum recommended size 90cm [35in] square) conforming to British Standard BS 6575 will be suitable for use in the home, but not all types can be reused.

Don't use damp tea towels instead. They may temporarily suffocate the flames, but all too often the heat in the pan dries the cloth, burns through and you could end up with a very serious fire. In one home I know a damp towel was used and the heat burnt a hole in the frying pan and when the tea-towel had been burnt through, the flames shot up to the ceiling.

## How to use a fire blanket

- Hold the blanket securely and roll the corners around your hands to protect them.
- In case the heat from the flames is intense and the flames are blowing towards you, walk towards the fire shielding your body and face with the blanket.
- Hold your arms outstretched then slowly lay the blanket on top of the burning pan and in doing so you will exclude the oxygen. DO NOT REMOVE THE BLANKET.

- Turn off the heat and leave the blanket there. Then call the fire brigade and wait for them to make sure everything is safe. It is vital that you *do not remove the blanket* as the fat must have time to cool down. Otherwise it will re-ignite when you take the blanket off and the oxygen in the air comes into contact with the fat again.

Your local fire station will probably hold courses on how to use fire blankets and extinguishers in realistic situations. I'll never forget my own experience of having to put out a drum full of burning oil in a force six wind!

# Where should I put my fire-fighting equipment?

You should have a fire blanket and, if possible, a multi-purpose dry powder extinguisher in your kitchen — placed away from your cooker, hob or oven (preferably near the door) so that if there is a fire you can easily reach them.

It is also a good idea to have an extinguisher on your exit routes. This may mean putting an extinguisher on your first-floor landing and in your hallway. In general an extinguisher should be adjacent to an exit door.

# Smoke

SMOKE IS A KILLER and all smoke is dangerous.

About half the deaths from fire are the result of smoke inhalation and they often happen at night. Many people who do escape with their lives suffer *permanent damage to their lungs*.

Remember that it's not just the flames that kill. Over one thousand people die every year in the UK from the effects of fire.

Smoke is a combination of lethal gases, vapours and particles of partially burnt materials. It rises from a burning substance into the atmosphere. Whilst all fires release smoke, the amount and nature of the smoke depends on where the fire is and what has caught alight.

If a fire breaks out in a small enclosed space, such as a cupboard or a small room, then the amount of oxygen needed to feed the fire will be restricted and the result will be a very thick, heavy smoke. However, if the fire is in a well-ventilated area, for example in a room with an open window, it will produce a very fierce heat and burn more gases, vapours and particles and will produce a far lighter smoke.

## Gases released in a fire

Almost every material that burns produces gases that can kill you if inhaled.

*Carbon monoxide (CO)* is invisible and odourless and it spreads very quickly to all parts of the building and is often known as the silent killer.

*Carbon dioxide ($CO_2$)* is heavier than air and is also invisible and odourless and it has the same pervasive properties as carbon monoxide; it can ride on air currents and will reach even the remote parts of a building.

In a fire, these two gases will almost always be present but, with the use of modern materials, literally dozens of lethal gases can be released into the atmosphere. Gases such as ammonia, hydrogen cyanide, hydrogen chloride, chlorine, phosgene and sulphur dioxide are just some of the lethal gases that could be produced in a single fire.

Smoke is corrosive and an irritant. When people find themselves in a smoky atmosphere they become panicky and disorientated and often very confused.

## The hidden effects of smoke

Smoke damage to the lungs is the *main cause* of death to victims of fire. For example, people who suffer a single injury of even 80 degree burns can live, but victims who are affected by the combination of burns as minimal as 20 degrees and massive smoke inhalation will invariably die. Smoke can damage lungs beyond repair. The effects are horrible although not immediately visible. It can take several days for the damage to the lungs to become noticeable. And, unfortunately, even if the damage can be diagnosed immediately, nothing much can be done since the lungs will already have been damaged.

## Foam furniture

At long last the Government has woken up to the frightening hazards that foam materials can present. Now 'sub standard' foam (the sort that kills) is no longer allowed in furniture. Make sure that any furniture you buy conforms with the new *Furniture and*

*Furnishings (Fire)(Safety) Regulations 1988.*

Use a reliable dealer — don't be tempted by special cheap deals as they may be an attempt to offload potentially lethal stock.

The new foam is difficult to ignite and burns very slowly. The substandard foam is easily ignited and gives off lethal gases very quickly. When the concentration of hydrogen cyanide gas reaches as little as 300 parts per million, the effects are lethal. At this concentration,

• the first breath you take will temporarily cripple you
• the second breath will cause irreversible lung damage
• the third breath kills.

We simply can't afford to take this sort of risk.

# Early warning systems: smoke and heat detectors

## Harsh facts

• In 1987 only 10 per cent of UK homes had smoke detectors (compare this with 80 per cent of homes in the USA and Northern Europe).
• *For night-time fires, the time between ignition and discovery was typically 22 minutes or even longer.*
• Night-time fires are real killers. Smoke detectors can save lives.

Many of the 50,000 fires that occur in homes in this country every year would have claimed far fewer deaths and injuries if the inhabitants had been warned at an early stage. Smoke and heat detectors won't stop fires starting, but if they are properly installed they can give you an early warning of fire and increase your chances of escape.

Detectors needn't be expensive — many of the simple battery operated ones cost between £10 and £20. There are several designs, usually in white and they need not look unsightly or intrusive if you choose carefully.

There are two main types of detectors:

• *heat detectors* these are best to use in your kitchen since, as the name implies, they react to an increase in temperature around the detector
• *smoke detectors* these react to the smoke and gases coming from the fire and are more suit-

able for rooms other than the kitchen.

Smoke detectors also come in two types:

- *ionization smoke detectors* these work by measuring the change in an electrical current that occurs when smoke particles enter the detector
- *optical smoke detectors* inside these there is a small photoelectric cell and when the beam is disturbed by smoke particles the alarm is triggered.

Ionization detectors react quicker to hot, blazing flames, while optical detectors are better at detecting smouldering fires. Some detectors combine both devices in a single unit so that, in fact, you have the best of both worlds. However, in real-life situations these differences are marginal.

## Battery-operated detectors

The simplest smoke detectors are powered by self-contained batteries. These are fine provided you remember to change the battery *at least* annually and to test your detector regularly. Most of the detectors give out a little bleeping sound that sounds like a suffocating bat when the battery is getting low. Beware of this as I once spent several hours searching my house for what I was quite sure was an animal in distress only to discover that it was the intermittent bleep of my failing smoke detector.

Other smoke detectors can be powered from the mains and there are some very good 'home packs' specially made for the domestic market. The British Standard Number is BS 5446 for smoke detectors.

---

## Four points to remember when positioning detectors

- Make sure your smoke detector is fixed to the ceiling at least 30 cm(12 in) away from a light or a wall. Place it centrally if possible. Some detectors are specially designed for wall mounting —place them between 15-30 cm (6-12 in) below the ceiling.
- Beware of fitting a detector above a heater or an air conditioning vent.
- Don't put a detector in a bathroom where it may be triggered by steam and condensation.
- Make sure you can reach your detector fairly easily so that you can test it regularly. Stairwells can be hazardous!

# How many do I need? Where should I put them?

You need at least one and probably more depending on the size of your house.

## In a bungalow

Position a detector in the corridor between the sleeping and the living accommodation. Put one in the living room and any other room that is unoccupied at night.

Don't use a smoke detector in your kitchen because you will find that the fumes from burning toast and frying bacon will constantly set it off — your children will become so complacent about hearing the warning alarm that they might not react when there is a real fire. Ideally every room except the kitchen should have a smoke detector.

## Houses with a first floor

You should have one detector fixed to the ceiling of your downstairs hall and another on the first floor landing. In this way you will be warned of a fire on either floor. Then, you should consider putting detectors in the unoccupied rooms at night — for example your living room and dining room and certainly your loft, cellar and spare room if you have one. In the diagram overleaf

you can see where the real priority areas are and then, if funds permit, what the ideal situation would be. If anyone smokes in the bedroom (a highly dangerous habit) then, of course, a smoke detector in that room is absolutely essential and should be included in your priority plan.

## Houses with a second floor

Here again it is a simple question of extending the smoke detectors in the stairways and bedrooms if possible. Also, it is very sensible to put at least a half-hour fire resisting door at the bottom of the stair way up to the second floor in order to give the Fire Brigade more time to rescue anyone who is trapped on the second floor. A half-hour fire door will do exactly that, it will prevent the fire from burning through the door for up to 30 minutes and, if it is correctly fitted, it will also keep out most of the smoke.

If you are in any doubt about what to do and how best to protect yourself — telephone your local fire prevention office: particularly if you have any long corridors (of 15 m (49 ft) or more) it is important to get advice from the experts.

Where to place your smoke detectors

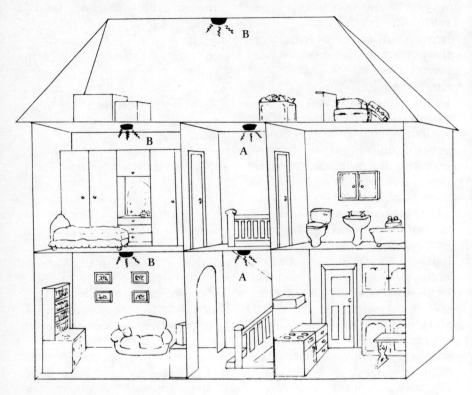

*Key:*  A = priority
        B = highly recommended

# Causes of fire

Let's think of a few simple ways in which a fire can start:

- cigarette smoking: carelessness with smoking materials is the cause of one quarter of Britain's yearly total of fires in buildings. Use *metal* waste bins not plastic or straw and always empty ashtrays down the loo last thing at night
- faulty electrical equipment or over-loaded circuits
- fat or other kitchen fires
- unguarded fires: *Note*: the law in England states that if a child

under 12 (in Scotland, under seven) is allowed into a room with an unguarded fire or heater and is severely burned, the person in charge is liable to prosecution and a fine)

- there are also some particularly lethal chemicals that we use every day. For example, did you realize that, if you use an aerosol, many of the solvents involved are highly flammable? If you are using your hairspray, for example, and you are smoking a cigarette you could find yourself holding a blow torch that is rapidly incinerating your hair. Aftershave is another highly flammable substance (with or without an aerosol). Do you remember the very sad story of the man who actually set his face on fire by smoking an early morning cigarette just after he had shaved and liberally applied the after-shave?
- gas: if you smell gas, put out cigarettes, don't use matches or a naked flame, and — something many people forget — DON'T OPERATE ELECTRICAL SWITCHES, either off or on (they could cause an explosion), open doors and windows to get rid of the gas, check to see that a gas tap has not been left on accidently or if a pilot light has gone out (if not, there is probably a gas leak: turn off the supply at the meter and call the Gas Board).

An automatic gas leak monitoring device that only needs to be plugged into a normal 13 amp socket has been developed for domestic use. The 'Gas Alert' emits a powerful alarm signal whenever combustible gas is present in the air above a pre-set safe level. It costs between £30 and £40 but if you have gas in your home you should consider installing one of these (see Useful Addresses, page 164).

Don't take chances, at home or in the street. If you suspect a gas leak phone the Gas Board. Keep the emergency number handy!

### Remember
- Don't let children play with matches or lighters.
- Watch chip pans and don't over-fill them.
- Check heaters — make sure nothing has been left to dry on or near them or that they are too near a piece of furniture or anything flammable.
- Don't dry tea-towels above the cooker.
- Some glues and multipurpose adhesives are highly inflammable — follow the instructions on the packet carefully and ventilate the room well.
- Keep lamps well away from curtains and bedding.

**At night**

- Make sure everything is switched off and unplug your television.
- Empty all the ashtrays into the loo last thing at night — nothing burns round the 'S' bend.
- Never smoke in bed.
- Close the doors to any rooms downstairs.

# Toys

Cuddly toys that are made in England must conform to the British Safety Standard number BS 5665. However, unfortunately, there are many imported cuddly toys that come from places all over the world which have not been tested to this standard. Some of these toys are *very very dangerous*. I have seen one child in hospital as a result of playing with his cap gun near his cuddly teddy. The spark from the cap gun set light to the teddy and, within seconds, the child suffered appalling burns. If your child does get given a cuddly toy that doesn't appear to have any British Standard on it then there is a simple way to test it:

- turn teddy upside down
- take a wet tea towel and wrap it round his foot (do this in the garden if possible and have a bowl of water by your side)
- light a match and, on the small area underneath the foot, light the fur (if it is safe the fur should just go out and there will be har-

dly any damage to your bear, but if the toy is dangerous, the fur will ignite and you must immediately plunge teddy's foot into the bowl of water)

- *Warning:* make sure there are no children in the area.

    *Only expose a very small area* of the foot to the flame and surround it with a very damp tea towel as some of these fabrics can flare up instantly.

I hope that this will not have caused a major riot in your home and that your children, like mine, will realize how important it is to make sure that their playthings are really safe.

I very much hope that no one who reads this book will ever be involved in a fire, but the likelihood is that some of you will. The important thing is to minimize the risk by following the advice set out in this chapter so far. BUT, of course you are still at risk — you must have a *well pre-*

Make sure your cuddly toys are safe

*pared plan of action* in case you are involved in a fire — especially at night.

Any of us may have a fire and have to leave the house in a hurry, ... in the dark ... in smoke ... in a panic ... so, *be sure that your escape route is safe and clear of obstacles*.

Check the children's rooms when you've kissed them goodnight and make sure they can get from their bed to the door without battling with their lego castle or a mini train set.

## Planning and practising your escape

Talk about fire with your children and show them why you think it's sensible to work out what to do just in case there is a fire.

Talk about how you would evacuate your home, perhaps over breakfast, and discuss the various routes that you would take. This is where lots of questions like 'What would you do if you were sleeping on the top floor and the fire alarm went off?' and 'Do you think you could get out of the house in the middle of the night if there weren't any lights on?' are very helpful. Of course, if your children are very young then this is an exercise you'll have to do for yourself, but, certainly, six-year-olds and upwards can easily be involved in practising getting out and they very often take great delight in making it a fun game. My boys practise escaping with blindfolds whilst I hover in the background to make sure that there are no accidents on the way.

Teach your children to practise getting out in case of a fire

# When fire strikes

I stayed in a busy hotel in Leeds recently. The fire alarm sounded at 2.00 am. I was downstairs within about 30 seconds, but I was appalled to watch the snail-like response from the other guests. The next person to arrive, 3 minutes later, was a business man who had stayed to get dressed (complete with tie) and was busily cramming papers into a briefcase. It took 10 minutes for-most people to assemble down-stairs to wait for the fire brigade and only 60 per cent of guests actually left their rooms. *Com-placency kills.*

Let's now consider that the worst has happened. You've woken up to the sound of the alarm of one of your smoke detec-tors or, worse still, you wake up smelling smoke.

## What should you do?

First, don't hesitate—time is of the essence. Go straight to your children. If you are able to wrap them in a dressing gown all well and good but the important thing is to GET OUT QUICKLY AND WITHOUT PANIC. If you find the exit route is smoky, crouch down or crawl if necessary as there is always cleaner air close to floor level. For example, at Banstead hospital, one wing was burnt so badly that it was never rebuilt; the walls and ceiling were com-pletely blackened, but there was a small area — about 15 cm (6 in) high at the bottom of the walls that was completely untouched. That was where the smoke had not reached and where the clean air had still been available.

Don't try to find any valuables; don't waste time bringing teddy too — just concentrate on leaving your house. Take your children with you and get out of the house and call the Fire Brigade from a neighbour's house.

If you and your children really have practised this evacuation procedure and talked about what you would do in case of a fire, then you should find that getting out becomes almost automatic so that you really can do it in your sleep.

## If you suspect a fire behind a closed door . . .

- Is there smoke escaping bet-ween the sides of the door frame and under the door?
- Is the door handle or door hot? Test with the back of your hand — this way, if you do burn your-self you still have the use of the palm of your hand to open the

other doors and escape. If the answer to either of these questions is yes, DON'T OPEN THE DOOR because, if you do, you will fuel the fire with fresh oxygen and you may well be blasted with a sheet of flames and hot smoke. This is called a 'flash over.'

## 'Flash over'

Many fires begin without any visible flames in confined spaces and they may go on smouldering for quite some time before any sign is noticed. Then, quite suddenly, the fire will burst out of its relatively small pocket of local heat and take hold of the whole building in a matter of minutes.

How does this happen? Well, when the fire is smouldering in a confined space there will be a gradual buildup of heat and there will be a number of vapours and gases that are being given off which can't escape. This means that there is a buildup of pressure in the room. This pressure, as well as the heat, may be what causes a window or a partition to collapse and brings the heated inside atmosphere into contact with the air outside. When the inside atmosphere reaches the right temperature and the right concentration of air to vapour, it ignites explosively and is hence called a flash over.

## If you can't escape

If the fire has progressed too far and the smoke is intense then you may not be able to escape. Try to reach the children and stay in one room — preferably one at the *front* of the house so that it's easier for you to attract attention and for the Fire Brigade to reach you. If you are all in one room this will help the children who, like you, will be very frightened. The rescuing firemen will only need to brave the route to one room. Then:

- close the door
- block any gaps with wet towels or bedding
- if possible phone for the Fire Brigade
- open the window and shout for help.

### Calling the Fire Brigade
As soon as your children are capable of using the telephone you should teach them how to call the emergency services. Make absolutely sure that they know *they must give their address* if they are phoning an emergency service and, if possible, they should also give the telephone number that they are calling from. This may all sound far too much for a small child to take in but I can assure you that it can and does work and you will be surprised at the com-

petence of your own children.

My boys had great fun visiting our local fire station and learning exactly how to make a 999 call. We often practise it at home using 'make believe' telephones!

I hope this has covered a subject that fills a great many of us with alarm and panic. It is one of the areas that I find most frightening and one which I think we don't take nearly seriously enough. If you still have any worries or queries about the safety of your own house in a fire, talk to the Fire Prevention Officer at your local Fire Station. Fire Officers are, in my experience, exceptionally helpful and friendly people and they appreciate being asked for help *before* any accidents occur.

---

Heed the simple motto:
- GET OUT
- GET THE FIRE BRIGADE OUT
- STAY OUT

---

*Note:* see useful BS numbers at the end of the book for information on fireguards, heaters, nightdresses, electrical and gas appliances, etc.

# CHAPTER 4

# SAFETY OUTDOORS

Whatever the weather, everyone enjoys being outside so, let's make sure that we get the most enjoyment — safely.

## Safety in the garden

### Harsh facts

- In 1986 67,000 children (under 15) in Great Britain needed medical attention as a result of an accident in the garden.

As you can see from this statistic, gardens aren't as safe as you might think. There are a number of areas that can cause accidents if simple precautions aren't taken.

### Climbing frames

Do you have any wooden or metal climbing frames? If so, check that these are all in good repair, that the metal frames aren't rusting and that the wooden frames are smooth and won't cause splinters. Most climbing frames come with special fixtures to make sure that the frames can be attached to the ground and won't topple over. Make sure that your climbing frames are on even ground and that if a child is playing on one end, it will not tip up. The ground underneath the frame must be soft so that if he falls off he won't hurt himself. Don't forget that hard-baked earth can be just as hard as concrete (which can be lethal.) Dig a shallow pit and line it with wooden boards. Fill it with woodchips. Result: a cheap safe area under the swing or climbing frame that could save your children from a disaster.

There are also some excellent impact-absorbing surfaces, including plastic tiles. If you need advice on what to use, contact either the Safety in Playgrounds Action Group or Fair Play for Children (see Useful Addresses, pages 164 and 165).

## Lawnmowers

Are you lucky enough to have a lawn in your garden? Take care because cutting the lawn can be a hazardous task. Any sticks or stones in the grass may be flung into the air while you are using the lawnmower.

Make sure that no one is within at least 10 metres (33 ft) of the mower and wear a visor yourself to protect your eyes. If you are using any mower with a hard blade (plastic or otherwise) always wear a pair of strong shoes or safety boots so that you and your toes don't part company.

## Gates

Does your garden lead out onto the main road? If it does, make sure that you have a self-closing gate that can be firmly secured. If your child is very young make sure he cannot open it.

## Poisonous plants

There are several deadly plants that are commonly found in gardens.

*Lily of the valley* The ripe berries are extremely poisonous. Also, if the picked flowers are put in a vase, the flower water will be very toxic to an inquisitive child who tries to drink it.

*Foxglove* This plant is very poisonous.

*Giant hogweed* As its name suggests, it is a very long plant. It grows up to 3 – 5 metres (9.8–16 ft), tall and has white flowers. It is also found in waste areas and has become quite an established garden escapee! The juice in the stems causes very severe blisters. Children should NEVER cut the stems to use them as telescopes etc.

*Monkshood* This has tall spikes of blue to purple flowers. Just a very small amount of this plant can kill.

*Larkspur* All varieties of this plant are very poisonous. It has purple/blue flowers.

*Laburnum trees* These are the commonest cause of plant poisoning. The seeds can be deadly.

Lily of the valley

Foxglove

Giant hogweed

Monkshood

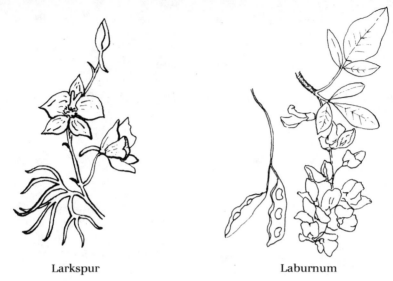

Larkspur                 Laburnum

Poisonous plants commonly found in the garden

## Pesticides and weedkillers

Are you plagued by weeds and pests and have resorted to using weedkiller or pesticides? Make sure that you follow the instructions on the label and lock them away after use.

## Ladders

How many of you have ladders stored in the garden? Children love climbing ladders, so, if you don't want an accident to happen, please make sure that they are stored well away and that the children know that they must never climb the ladder without an adult being present. Teach by

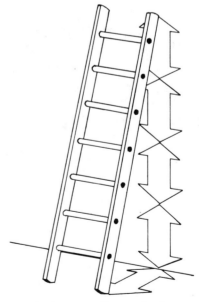

The 'one out, four up' rule

example too — follow the ladder code yourself.

*Remember:*

- the 'one out, four up' rule: for every four feet (1.2 m) up the wall the ladder should be one foot (0.3 m) out — away from the wall.
- face the ladder when climbing up or down
- never use an unsound ladder
- place the ladder on a firm, level base
- fit your ladder with non-slip feet.

# In the playground

## Harsh facts

- On average there are 150,000 serious injuries each year from playground accidents .. that's 3,000 a week!
- 80 per cent of these happened even though the children were being supervised
- 37 per cent occurred on climbing frames
- 47 per cent of the serious injuries were head injuries
- 14 per cent involved broken arms or fingers
- 11 per cent involved broken legs

There are a number of excellent playgrounds, with imaginative ideas that have been thoughtfully planned to not only to provide a great deal of fun, but also to provide a safe playing environment. *However*, there are still some very dangerous playgrounds with swings, climbing frames, etc., built over hard surfaces, and slides where, if you are light, you may well slide off the end at a speed that could quite easily result in disaster.

All playground equipment has to comply with BS 5696. This states that children should not be allowed to have a free fall of 2.4 metres (8 ft) for any piece of equipment and that safety surfacing is 'strongly recommended' for any equipment that makes falls possible. Plastic tiles and woodchips are just two of the surfaces that can be used.

In a survey carried out by the Consumers' Association Magazine *Which* in 1987, more than 70 per cent of the playgrounds visited had swings, slides and climbing frames built on concrete or tarmac — both surfaces causing serious injuries to children who fall.

Other problems they found were:

- broken glass and litter
- at least one third of all the roundabouts, swings, etc., were not properly maintained
- many had broken or rusty handrails and frames that had simply been painted over.

Fortunately, thanks to Esther Rantzen's initiative, there is a move afoot amongst many local authorities to improve the safety in their playgrounds radically. If you feel that your local playground is unsafe and contact with the local council produces no result then contact the Safety In Playgrounds' Action Group, which campaigns for improved safety for children in playgrounds (see Useful Addresses, page 165).

Similarly, if your school playground worries you, speak to the headteacher who may well be sympathetic to your problem and be only too delighted to have support from some of the parents when approaching the school governors for funds to improve the situation.

Finally, if you do find a safe playground — and there certainly are some very good ones around —then make sure your child is wearing suitable clothing, some sensible shoes for climbing (not Wellingtons) and no loose clothing or scarves that could get caught up.

# Sports injuries

## Harsh facts

- In 1987 there were about 9,000 accidents in schools, half of which were sports related.

Although I'm very keen for my boys to play football and rugby, cricket, tennis and anything else they might want to try, like any mother I always have a lurking fear in the back of my mind that they may be badly injured.

Although we don't hear very much about it, a number of children are seriously injured when playing sport. Many schools now are advising parents to insure their children against accidents.

## Rugby

New laws for rugby in New Zealand have produced a dramatic reduction in injuries to players. With the new laws (particularly relating to scrums and mauls) the necks broken in the scrum fell from 15 a year to 1. At present the International Rugby Football Board has refused to adopt the New Zealand laws. Must we wait for even more children to be injured or even crippled before the law is changed?

## Other sports

There are a number of things that you can do to minimize injury risk and it might also be sensible to talk to the school and check that they are aware of the risk-factors involved. It is vital for sports teachers to have been properly trained as good tuition produces safer play. Here are some things that you can do:

- make sure your child has the correct protective clothing. This may include a custom-made mouthguard (rugby, hockey, etc.) Ideally this should be fitted by a dentist and it should be checked regularly as children's mouths do change. Not only does it give protection to irreplaceable teeth, it also significantly reduces head trauma and lessens the possibility of any concussion. Protective clothing may also include an eye shield (squash), a thigh pad, box and shin guards depending on the sport.

- make sure that your child has suitable kit. Shirts, shorts (trousers in the case of cricket) and shoes must be the right size and be comfortable. Trousers that are too long can cause the child to trip and clothing which is too tight restricts movement and can rub. For rugby, etc., make sure your son wears a comfortable pair of trunks underneath his shorts rather than a jock strap. A jock strap can compress the testicles against the pubic bone if they are hit.

- make sure that watches, medals, chains, etc., are all removed before the game and, certainly, if it is a team game, no earrings should be worn.

- chewing gum! It is very, very unsafe for your child to chew anything whilst he is playing a game — he could easily choke.

## Playing facilities

In the case of team games it is always advisable to check that the pitch is free of dangerous debris and that there are no potholes or rough lumps and bumps. Rugby goalposts should be covered with some form of protective padding at the bottom and any marker flags should be made from a lightweight flexible material. Nowadays few schools use creosote pitch markings as creosote is a toxic chemical and can be carcinogenic, but, if your school does, suggest it changes to a chalk solution. Finally, make sure that your child is up to date with his tetanus injections as he will be in contact with soil or perhaps bird or animal droppings on the grass that may infect his bloodstream if he is cut (see Chapter 8).

# Bonfires and fireworks

## The fireworks code

- Keep fireworks in a closed box, take them out one at a time and put the top back on at once.
- Follow the instructions on each firework carefully — read them by torch light — never a naked flame.
- Light the end of the fireworks fuse at arm's length — preferably with a safety firework lighter or fuse wick.
- Never throw fireworks.
- Stand well back.
- Never return to a firework once lit — it may go off in your face.
- Never put fireworks in your pocket.
- Keeps pets indoors.
- NEVER FOOL WITH FIREWORKS.

## Harsh facts

In 1987:
- 960 people were injured in Great Britain by fireworks in a four week period in October and November
- 312 of these injuries were eye injuries
- 540 (over half) of the total number of injuries were to children under 16.

These are only the reported injuries — in reality the total number is probably far far greater.

I love bonfires and still get enormous pleasure from baking potatoes in the embers, toasting large chunks of bread or better still marshmallows. If you are having a bonfire, whether or not it's November the Fifth, keep the following advice well in mind:

- choose your site carefully. Remember the wind may change and flames may blow in any direction
- check the bonfire before lighting it, make sure that no animal or child is near (one child died because he was hiding in the bonfire when it was lit)
- build it well clear of buildings, garden sheds, firework display areas, fences and hedges
- keep a bucket of water or hosepipe handy just in case
- never put fireworks onto bonfires even if they are duds
- never use flammable liquids to start the fire
- never burn dangerous rubbish — aerosols, foam furniture, etc. Aerosols can explode and the foam may give off toxic fumes. Beware of concrete encrusted items such as discarded fence posts. The concrete can explode and cause dreadful injuries
- don't leave your bonfire unattended. Someone should have the time to supervise it until it is consumed. If it has to be left, dampen it down and rake out the embers
- make sure no children will be playing anywhere near.

# Going to a friend's house

This is where you will have to employ a great deal of tact not to upset your friends, but also to make sure that there are no special hazards involved. Here are some of the things that you should be establishing before the visit:

- does your friend know whether or not your child can swim? If he can't, send him with arm bands if they are likely to go swimming and warn your friend that he will need constant supervision
- are there gates across the stairs if your child is still at the crawling or toddling stage?
- are there any ornaments low enough that your child might pick them up, swallow them or break them?
- is the floor very slippery? If so make sure he is wearing shoes with a good grip
- will they be going on a bicycle or tricycle ride? Children are much safer riding their own cycles so take his own if you can
- if you have any *special* worries then have the courage to tell your friend so that she or he can be specially aware of them when your child is there
- Is your child allergic to any par-

ticular food, animal or insect? — If he is make sure your friend knows

• if possible, leave a telephone number where you can be contacted in an emergency.

Remember too that when someone comes to stay with your child that you must warn *them* if there is anything a little bit unsafe in *your* house.

Under the Occupier's Liability Act you have a duty to take reasonable care that your visitors are safe. 'Visitors' can include outside contractors such as builders, washing machine repairmen (a frequent sight in my house!),

home helps, district nurses and anyone else you have invited in. Similarly, if you employ someone at home, a cleaner, gardener, nanny or secretary, for example, you must also ensure that your home is reasonably safe for the purpose for which they are there. If you know of any problem areas, warn your visitors *before* they find out the hard and perhaps, painful, way. You may have a wobbly banister that everyone in the household knows about (and, in fact, is going to be mended next week), but someone new coming into the house could be taken unawares.

## In the woods

Going for a walk in the woods is such good fun that really no one wants to bother to think about any special safety precautions. However, there are one or two things that it's worth remembering and I don't think they should spoil the enjoyment of your walk one little bit.

If it starts to rain you will naturally shelter under a tree hoping that the rain will pass. However, if it starts to thunder as well do not stand under a tree. Trees are very good conductors and the most sensible thing

would be to stand in the middle of an open field and get wet rather than risk being struck by lightning under a tree.

If you are walking in the bracken or anywhere where there might be an adder or, if you are abroad, any other sort of poisonous snake, don't wear open-toed sandals. Teach your children not to touch fungi as there are so many poisonous varieties around and children often tend to put their fingers in their mouths. I have three sisters and we are all avid fungus eaters:

we were taught at a very early age which were poisonous and which were edible. However, unless you are absolutely sure it is better to teach that, when in doubt, a fungus could easily give you an upset stomach and at worst could kill you.

There are lots of edible berries in the woods: blackberries, wild strawberries and raspberries are all to be found on the Sussex Downs where I spent a great deal of my childhood, but there are also berries that are deadly and children should never eat any berry unless they have checked first with an adult who knows which are edible and which are poisonous. Not only are some berries poisonous, but there are also some *very* poisonous *plants* that grow wild in England. Here are some you should be particularly wary of (for a more comprehensive list of these and deadly fungi see the Appendix on page 161):

*Yew* A yew tree has pink berries that look very appetizing, but the seeds inside these are deadly and the leaves too are very poisonous. When bow and arrows were the weapons of the day, yew trees were needed to make excellent longbows but, as yew leaves are so poisonous, these trees were planted in the church graveyards out of reach of cattle.

Common poisonous plants found in woods

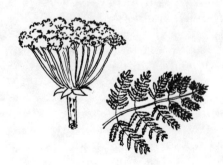

Yew                                    Hemlock

Wild arum

Deadly nightshade

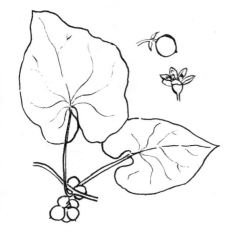

Black bryony

Thornapple

Henbane

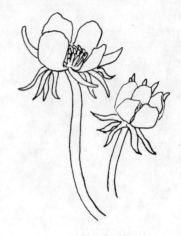

Winter aconite

Spurge laurel

*Hemlock* This plant looks very similar to cow parsley. It is often found near streams and on waysides and is very poisonous. Children should be warned against making blowpipes or whistles from the hollow stems.

*Wild arum* (sometimes known as 'Lords and Ladies') This has clusters of red berries that can cause diarrhoea if eaten and a nasty skin rash if handled.

*Deadly nightshade* This has black berries that are extremely poisonous.

*Black bryony* This, despite its name, has bright scarlet berries. It is often found in hedgerows and could make a child very ill.

*Thornapple* All parts of this are deadly. The seeds are found in a spiny (thorny) pod.

*Henbane* This wild flower is often found near the sea in sandy soil. This is what Dr Crippen used to murder his wife in 1901!

*Winter aconite* This is often found in woods and flowers in early spring. It is poisonous.

*Spurge laurel* An erect shrub 40–100cm (16-39in) high with evergreen leaves and black poisonous berries.

## Bird watching

The Isle of Skye has a very rocky coastline. My parents knew that their four daughters were reasonably sensible and well trained in the various hazards that abounded, but, even so, they made sure that we never went off on our own, but always went in pairs. It was all too easy to slip on a wet rock and fall and hit our heads and it is often very difficult to find someone who has fallen into the bracken. If you are going bird watching the last thing you want to do is to wear bright clothes — every bird in the place would fly away — but it does make it even more difficult for the person who is looking for you to see you. The golden rule is to *stay together and let someone know where you are going and the latest time by which you will return.*

# Holidays

## Holiday accommodation

Whenever you stay somewhere new it's sensible to find out about the safety precautions there —and to check for any hazards.

In a hotel find out what the fire precautions are, where your nearest exit route is and what the alarm system sounds like. It may be the familiar bell but sometimes it sounds like a siren! I always count the number of bedroom doors between my room and the exit door to the staircase so that I could find my way out in the dark if I had to.

There have been some horrific accidents to children in hotel lifts when on holiday in some countries in Europe. Some lifts do not have doors and it is possible for a child's limb to be trapped in the space between the shaft and the lift. Some children have sadly lost an arm as a result. Check the facilities on arrival.

If the hotel has a swimming pool, make sure your children know which are the shallow and deep areas and follow the Water Wise code given in Chapter 5, on page 87.

Spend a little time looking for hazards, such as scalding hot water, treacherous stairways and balconies. Warn your children of the dangers.

## Skiing holidays

Two of the main hazards for children on a skiing holiday are too much sun and too much cold. Small children have difficulty in regulating their temperature and. they can easily suffer from hypothermia (see Chapter 6 on first aid, page 107) without anyone noticing. Normally they will look pale and ill, although very young children may become rosy cheeked, and gradually become sleepy and lethargic. Be very careful to avoid this happening: make sure your children are well wrapped up in warm waterproof clothing, with boots that will protect their feet and a hat. A hat is very important since one third of the body's heat escapes through the top of the head.

The ultraviolet rays in ski resorts are particularly strong because they are reflected off so many surfaces and because of the altitude. Use a good sunblock cream to protect your children's skin. I have seen children in abso-lute misery whose ears and eyelids and noses have been so badly burned that they blistered. Don't let this happen to your child.

Perhaps you will remember the terrible tragedy when four teenagers fell more than 70 metres (250 ft) to their death while they were on a school trip in the Austrian Alps. Some newspaper reports suggested that the boys were wearing boots with smooth soles and, when they wandered off the path and started to slip, they couldn't stop themselves as they fell over the cliff.

It is essential to stick to the safe routes and not stray away from the group and it is vital that everyone wears the correct clothing. Not only is it important to have the right shoes or boots but also to make sure that your children don't wear 'make-do' ski suits that are made of plastic and provide no resistance to slipping if they should fall. Most ski suits now are made of an anti-slip material. If they are not practical then thick cotton trousers that have been waterproofed would be much safer than plastic waterproofs over the top of ordinary trousers.

If your child is joining a school party, talk to the organizers and make sure that they are well aware of the potential hazards and how to avoid them.

# School outings and day trips

Here is a list of questions to ask the school before the trip. Make sure you are happy with the answers to your questions before signing the consent form. (Depending on the outing you may decide that not all of these questions are relevant.)

- What is the ratio of staff to pupils on this trip?
- What are the arrangements should anyone — staff or pupil — become unwell?
- Will one of the staff members be a trained first aider?
- What special hazards may my child encounter?
- Will there be any unsupervised activities?
- Does any member of staff have relevant experience and/or qualifications?
- What mode of transport will be used?
- Have any of the staff visited this place previously?
- Do the staff have emergency contact numbers for the parents or guardians of the pupils on this trip?
- Are staff aware of any special needs of the pupils concerned, such as allergies, medication, fear of heights, etc?
- Is all the necessary equipment (life jackets, wet suit, or whatever) provided?
- Is the party adequately insured?

For overnight stays a far more comprehensive questionaire is necessary and you will need to spend time talking to the staff involved until you feel confident that there are no loopholes in the safety net.

# Children and farms

There are many children who live on farms or whose parents are involved in horticulture, fruit-growing, dairy-farming and market-gardening.

If a child is 13 years old he is then eligible to work part-time on a farm, but there are also many who perform tasks on farms who are not 'employed' in the strict legal sense. They may be helping their parents as a matter of course or working for pocket money.

The statistics make grim reading:

- 120 children were killed as a result of agricultural accidents between 1977 and 1985.

Amongst the under 13 age group:

- 27 fatalities involved tractors
- 16 fatalities involved drowning in slurry pits, cesspits or other water hazards that weren't properly fenced off or guarded and the majority of these accidents were to the under fives
- 12 involved children being crushed by falling or over-turned objects.
- over two thirds of the fatal accidents to children in agriculture occur to children at play, of which one half are under five years old.

There are no reliable statistics for non-fatal accidents to children but they are thought to be high.

Although your child may not have direct access to a farm, market garden or whatever, he may well be taken on a school visit or with friends or perhaps stay there for a holiday so, very briefly, let's look at this dangerous area.

A new code of practice concerning children and agriculture was brought out in May 1988 by The Health and Safety Commission.

There are some very specific points about the employment of children on farms but some of the more general recommendations are:

- employers should warn children about any hazardous areas and make sure that all doors, fences, guards and covers leading to hazardous areas, etc., are kept closed. Also places like grain pits should now be properly guarded
- under the safety regulations, a child under the age of 13 must not ride on, or drive, tractors or other farm machines. Any person who causes or permits a child to do so is guilty of an offence
- a child is now not allowed to enter fruit or grain stores that are enclosed in order to retain an oxygen-deficient atmosphere. Also, in general, he can not enter a silo or storage bin or a slurry pit, cesspit or tank
- animals with newborn young can be very protective and will attack anyone who comes too near. For this reason children are now forbidden to enter an enclosed yard, pen or stall occupied by a bull, boar or stallion or a cow, sow or mare with newborn young without adequate supervision
- a child may not lift any-

thing that is too heavy or likely to cause him an injury, nor may he use any ladder unless it is bound and properly maintained and either held in position or securely placed.

You may think that much of the above doesn't apply to you or your children, but if I give you three examples of the sort of accidents that have happened, I think you will see how very easily tragedies do occur.

*'A girl of three was killed when she was knocked down by a large wooden box holding harvested potatoes which was being moved by a tractor in the field where her mother was working.'*

*'A nine-year-old visitor to a farm was killed in a tower silo. He was found with his clothing caught up in the machinery. The hatch doorway to the silo had been left off for easy access.'*

*'A girl of four received fatal injuries when a stack of hay bales in which she was playing collapsed on top of her.'*

*Source:* Approved Code of Practice and Guidance Notes. Preventing Accidents to Children in Agriculture. Reproduced with the kind permission of the Controller of Her Majesty's Stationery Office.

I don't think that I need give more examples.

If you are directly or indirectly involved in agriculture, you have

Never go near a bull

a great many duties, not only to your children, but to the children of employees and visitors, to school parties and to people who are just out for a stroll in the countryside. However, the responsibility for safety is *not* just the farmer's. The best-run farms are still full of hazards and, even with all these new recommendations, it is still very possible for serious accidents to occur. Teach your children about the hazards and how easily accidents can happen and make sure that they are properly supervised.

---

### Eight safety points for children to remember when visiting a farm

- always ask the farmer or manager for permission to visit and find out which areas are out of bounds
- never play *with* or *on* any mechanical equipment
- closed gates and fences are there for a good reason — stay on the right side of them
- keep well away from any moving vehicle or equipment
- never go near an animal and its young without first checking with an adult
- never go near a bull
- don't stand behind an animal — you may frighten it and be kicked!
- don't wander off on your own. Children are often too small to be seen by the drivers of large farmyard machinery. Stay close and stay safe.

---

Don't send your child with a school party to visit or stay on a farm unless you have first checked with the teachers the safety precautions and the level of supervision. All too often the teachers themselves have been inadequately briefed and may be unaware of some of the dangers.

# Building sites

Beware! There have been some terrifying accidents to children on building sites. The construction industry has embarked upon a campaign to reduce such deaths and injuries, which includes

Building sites and children just do not mix

educating children about the dangers by showing them round sites and pointing out the numerous hazards.

The Health and Safety Executive has issued guidance notes to help prevent accidents and these include the erection of a fence at least 2 metres (6.5 ft) high, which cannot easily be climbed. It also has a film called 'Building Sites Bite' that teaches children about the dangers of playing around a building site.

Contractors must be aware, but so must we. Children are naturally curious and sometimes a fence or scaffolding can, in fact, present quite a challenge to an enquiring child. Talk about how accidents can happen on these sites and don't be afraid to

include some of the real horror    that *building sites and children*
stories. Make it absolutely clear    *just do not mix.*

# CHAPTER 5

# SAFETY IN THE WATER

Over 600 people drown in the waters of the United Kingdom each year. As with so many of the accidents that are discussed in this book, many of these deaths could have been prevented by following a few simple rules.

RoSPA, The Royal Society for the Prevention of Accidents is a wonderful organization that, amongst other things, produces a wealth of information on all aspects of safety. Recently their Water and Leisure Department introduced a Water Wise Awareness Scheme which is aimed particularly at primary and nursery school children: although teenagers have the highest drowning figures, the scheme aims to make sure younger children grow up wiser and safer about water dangers.

Part of the Water Wise pro-

gramme is an Award Scheme whereby children are awarded certificates and badges when they have successfully completed the course. There is also a Rolf Harris video for schools to use and some fun but educational posters.

If you can, you should encourage your child's school to participate in the Scheme since it teaches simple but vital information. Basically the Water Wise code is:

- spot the dangers
- know the difference
- check new places
- take safety advice
- go with a grown-up
- learn how to help.

The good thing about this code is that it applies to all types of water situations.

*Spot the dangers* Water can look safe, but it can be dangerous. Learn to spot and keep away from dangers.

*Know the difference* You may be able to swim in a warm indoor pool, but that does not mean that you will be able to swim in cold outdoor water.

*Check new places* New places that you visit may have hidden dangers that you do not know about. Always ask somebody who knows.

*Take safety advice* Special flags and notices may warn you of danger. Know what the signs mean and do what they tell you.

*Go with a grown-up* Children should always go out with a grown-up, not by themselves. A grown-up can point out dangers or help if somebody gets into trouble.

*Learn how to help* You may be able to help yourself and others if you know what to do in an emergency.

Let's look at some of the areas where water safety is so important and you will see how this simple code applies.

# Leisure pools and public swimming pools

Of drownings in the United Kingdom, 3-5 per cent occur in swimming pools. The Sports Council, together with the Health and Safety Commission have produced a guide for public swimming pools that sets out clear guidelines for all the safety requirements.

You may remember the tragic story of the child who watched his uncle die in a pool in the Caribbean when an electric fault caused the pool to become 'live' and electrocuted him.

The new guidelines cover areas including:

• electrical installation
• design of the pool
• maintenance requirements
• equipment — including wave machines and water slides
• supervision arrangements
• pool water treatment and
• safety signs.

In 1987, RoSPA's National Water Safety Committee produced the National Water Safety Signs that, as you will see overleaf, graphically illustrate the instructions on the signs and should therefore be clearly understood by everyone, children and adults alike. Some of them apply to swimming pools — others to general water areas, ponds, the sea, etc.

'National Water Safety Signs 1987' posters are available in various sizes and materials to suit both indoor and outdoor locations. Full details about this and the Swimming Pool Users Code are available from The Royal Society for the Prevention of Accidents Water and Leisure Department (for their address, see page 165.) RoSPA has kindly allowed me to reproduce these signs overleaf.

Teach these signs to your children and make sure they understand them.

Play games, covering the bottom of the signs so that they can't read the writing and then ask questions. Discuss too where these signs might be used and *why* they might be needed. Remember:

- a red sign means 'do not'
- a yellow sign means 'a hazard'
- a blue sign means 'you must'
- a black and white sign means 'information'

You need to be especially careful in leisure pools and ensure that your children know exactly where it is safe for them to dive.

Wave machines can be very frightening to small children (and some adults!) They may suddenly find themselves out of their depth. Children with a hearing problem are also at risk as they may not be able to hear the warning bell before the waves begin. Someone should be close by to alert them.

## Swimming pool users

Here is the RoSPA Safety Code, this time applied to swimming pool users:

- spot dangers, take care — swimming pools can be hazardous. Water presents a risk of drowning and injuries can occur from hitting hard surrounds or from misuse of the equipment
- always swim within your ability and never swim after a heavy meal or after drinking alcohol. Avoid holding your breath and swimming long distances under water. Be especially careful if you have a medical condition such as epilepsy, asthma, diabetes or a heart condition
- check new places because every pool is different — always make sure you know how deep the water is, and check for other hazards such as diving boards, water slides and steep slopes into deeper water, etc.
- take safety advice and follow

Natio
Safety

## PROHIBITION SIGNS
### Activities

**No rowing**

**No water skiing**

**No fishing**

**No sailing**

*Right* Prohibition signs are red
and black on a white background

**No running**

**No windsurfing**

## WARNING SIGNS
### Water hazards

Warning signs are yellow and
black on a white background

### Activities

**DANGER Strong currents**

**DANGER Deep water**

**DANGER Sudden drop**

**Rowing area**

**Windsurfing area**

**Diving area**

**Motorised craft area**

## INFORMATION SIGNS
### Designated areas

**Snorkelling area**

**Fishing area**

Water
s 1987

No
sub-aqua

No
snorkelling

No
motorised craft

No
surfing

No
swimming

No
diving

DANGER
Shallow water

DANGER
Thin ice

MANDATORY
SIGNS
Protection

Water skiing
area

Surfing
area

Sailing
area

Lifejackets
must be worn

Swimming area

Sub-aqua area

*Above* Mandatory signs are
bright blue and white on a
white background

*Left* Information signs are
black and white

advice provided for your and others' safety. Avoid unruly behaviour, which can be dangerous — for instance, running along the side of the pool, ducking, acrobatics in the water, or shouting or screaming (which could distract attention from an emergency.) Always do as the lifeguards say, and remember that a moment of foolish behaviour could cost a life

• look out for yourself and other swimmers. It is safer to swim with a companion. Keep an eye open for others, particularly young children and non-swimmers

• learn how to help — if you see somebody in difficulty, get help immediately. In an emergency, keep calm and do exactly as you are told.

## Diving and snorkelling

*Snorkels* Never buy snorkels with a ping pong ball or valve attachment. They should have a simple tube. Valves can jam and balls can stick to the tube by suction and the snorkeller could choke.

*Masks* These should be made of toughened glass or plastic and if they cover the nose they must have a rubber pouch to enable you to equalize the pressure both inside and out. If you or your children can't do this the mask may squeeze onto the face and could even cause broken blood vessels in the eyes.

Snorkels and masks need to be used correctly if accidents are not to happen. Your local swimming club will put you in touch with a snorkelling group or you could contact the British Sub-Aqua Club (see Useful Addresses on page 163.)

*Diving* Never let your child (or anyone) dive wearing goggles. Blood vessels could burst in the eyes. Did you know that a normal ear drum can be perforated at a pressure of only 1.8 m (6 ft) under water? Thousands of people damage their ears through diving as a child. Often they will dive for pennies, even though it can be painful, as part of a game. Make sure your children never dive in deep water without proper training and that they tell you immediately of any ear problems, however minor. Unheeded damage to ears as a child can lead to all sorts of problems, especially with air travel in later life.

## Paddling pools

Remember, young children can drown in very small amounts of water and it is simply not safe to leave them alone anywhere near a paddling pool or any other water. I have been horrified at the number of parents who happily leave their three-year-old splashing around outside while they answer the telephone inside. It only takes a matter of minutes for a child to drown or suffer irreversible brain damage.

## Private swimming pools

Are you one of those lucky people who has their own swimming pool at the bottom of the garden? Take these simple precautions and you will be able to be much more relaxed about your children's and their friends' safety.

Make sure the pool is fenced off so that small children can't inadvertently fall in. If fencing it off is simply not practical — then make sure that when the pool is not in use it has a strong cover. This must be secured firmly to the pool edges so that it is impossible for anyone to fall onto it and drown or, as happened to one of my friends, for a small child to climb underneath the cover and then not be able to get out. (In this case, his mother found him before it was too late — you might not be so lucky).

When my son was only four years old he very nearly drowned in a swimming pool that was full

of people *and* had a lifeguard. There were adults all round the pool standing and talking. Not one of them noticed him underwater and, although he had fallen into the shallow end, his head did not once reach the surface. The adult with him had forgotten to put on his arm bands and had no idea that he had jumped into the shallow end. Fortunately he was rescued and suffered no ill effects. However, it showed me that you cannot afford to take *any* risks or to assume that a child will be sensible and think before he jumps! There should always be an adult with your children when they are swimming whether in your own pool, a public pool or at a friend's. Even children who can swim well can easily hurt themselves when they are diving or just fooling around. A good swimmer should always be on hand. Whatever happens never ever let a child swim on his own. He may easily hit his head or get an attack of cramp or just become severely winded when diving or jumping in.

## Ponds

We have several ponds close by. Lovely as they are, they can easily become the site of an accident. Here again use the Water Safety Code and remember to treat any

An angered swan can break a child's arm

swans on the pond with great respect. An angered swan can break a child's arm. Any nesting birds will also be extremely aggressive to anyone who comes near their nests.

Ponds often look very inviting if it's a hot day and you're longing for a swim. Beware of water plants with long roots that can cut your legs and trap you — water lilies are one of the worst culprits. Play safe and only swim in places where swimming is authorized.

In winter, ice-covered ponds may *look* fun but no frozen surface is safe if the water below is of unknown depth. Play safe and keep well away.

## Small boats

I have spent many happy summers with my family sailing round the Isle of Skye in small boats, canoes and sailing boats. We have been thoroughly drilled in safety at sea but, even so, there is usually at least one slightly scary incident each holiday due to an unforeseen combination of events. One year we were out fishing and a fishing hook caught in my finger. No matter how hard I tried to remove the hook the barb just meant that it went in deeper and deeper. The safe thing to do is to leave the fish hook alone if it is not easily removable and go to the out-patients department of a hospital where they can help you and the hook part company. Another time I was hauling up a lobster pot but, unfortunately, a stinging jelly fish had left some of its tentacles on the rope. One of them flicked up into my eye and it was very painful. That unpleasant experience taught me to be cautious when hauling up ropes from the water.

Use the Safety Code and:

- make sure that you always wear proper life jackets (BS 3595) that will buoy you and your children up, should you capsize, with your heads above water
- never stand up in a boat or move quickly. You may capsize it
- don't go anywhere where there is a strong current and make sure that somebody on land knows that you are out in your boat.

Another excellent organization that produces invaluable advice is the Royal Life Saving Society, UK. The RLSS issues the following guidelines for use 'When in, on, or near water.'

- go with a friend
- tell someone where you are going and when you will be back
- read and obey notices and never cover them up
- report missing lifesaving equipment (or anyone taking or breaking it)
- choose an area patrolled by lifeguards
- always swim in line with the shore
- if you feel tired or cold get out of the water (cold can kill even strong swimmers)
- never go into the water after drinking alcohol
- don't use airbeds or inflatable toys on open water — wind and tides can quickly sweep them away
- learn from the experts how to enjoy water sports safely
- keep equipment in good working order and always wear an approved lifejacket or buoyancy aid when on the water
- avoid hazardous areas such as crumbling riverbanks, quarries and gravel pits with deep cold water and hidden dangers, fast-flowing water and ice-covered lakes, ponds and canals
- keep a watchful eye on toddlers near water
- If you fall and can't reach

safety, try to stay calm and regain your breath if the cold water has taken it away. If you can't stand up, turn over and float on your back. Attract attention by waving one arm and shouting for help.

If an accident does happen, the RLSS teaches five methods of rescue that should be considered. Keep to this order as the safest methods are first.

- *Reach* Lie flat and attempt to anchor yourself securely. Reach out as far as you are safely able. Look for something to extend your reach, such as a pole, an item of clothing, etc.
- *Throw* If the casualty is out of reach, stand well back and throw something that will float and enable a return to safety. Alternatively, use a rope to pull the person to safety.
- *Wade* Find something to test the depth of the water. Wade carefully no further than thigh-depth and use the aid to reach the casualty.
- *Swim* Find something that will float; swim carefully towards the casualty and throw the aid. Encourage a return to safety whilst keeping a safe distance between yourselves so that you cannot be grabbed and pulled under by a possibly panicked casualty.

- *Swim and Tow* If a casualty is unconscious a tow will be necessary. Swim out, watching the casualty; tow to safety as quickly as possible. Commence resuscitation if breathing has stopped.

There are some special flags that you should know which may be flying in the area where you and your children may wish to swim.

| Danger | Patrolled Bathing Area | Surfing |
|---|---|---|
| Red notice boards or flags mean it is unsafe to bathe. | Red over yellow flags mean the area is patrolled by lifeguards. | Black and white flags mark areas for surfing. It is unwise to bathe in these areas. |

Some other trouble spots include:

*Riverbanks* Keep away from slippery or crumbling banks along streams and rivers
*Canals and locks* Steep sides make it almost impossible to climb out, so keep well away from the edge
*Quarries and gravel pits* Deep

cold water and hidden hazards make these dangerous places to dive and swim

*Weirs* Keep well away — don't venture where rushing currents can sweep you away.

You and your family can learn more about Water Safety, lifesaving and resuscitation by contacting the Royal Life Saving Society (see page 165 for their address) who will be happy to forward free literature to you. Why not set the example and become a qualified lifesaver yourself?

# CHAPTER 6

# FIRST AID

Let's face it, however safe your home is, however vigilant you are, however wonderfully you educate your children, accidents do happen and a good basic knowledge of what to do in an emergency is essential.

Quite honestly it is not enough just to know what to do — it should become second nature so that, even if you yourself are in shock, your brain will switch on to autopilot and you will be able to save your child from serious harm.

Recently my 10-year-old son stopped breathing for what seemed like minutes although in fact was only seconds. My husband was away on business and my 6-year-old was the only other person in the house. Luckily, although I was very frightened, I managed to start his breathing again and call for help. It made me realize just how vital it was that my reactions were automatic as my brain felt very numb. Fortunately I didn't have to stop and think 'What do I do now?'

I have divided this chapter into several sections to make it easier for you to refer to.

*Section 1:*
How to cope with real disaster scenarios such as drowning, electric shock, poisoning, suffocation and burns.

*Section 2:*
How to cope with some very real problems caused by everyday occurrences (e.g. animal bites).

*Section 3:*
Some more unusual emergencies

that can be greatly helped by prompt action (e.g. losing a tooth, a finger or a toe).

Section 4:
What to have in your medicine cabinet or first aid kit.

# Section 1

Ideally you should attend a first aid course. The St John's Ambulance, the St Andrew's Ambulance Association and the British Red Cross Society all run excellent courses. Often they are held in the morning during school term-time but others are held in the evening, so there is usually a course available at a time that will suit you.

You will be taught by professionals and the course will include how to clear someone's airway, give mouth-to-mouth resuscitation (if the patient has stopped breathing) and external chest compressions (if the heart has stopped beating). These are often known as the ABC of recovery. You will also be shown the recovery position that ensures that the airway remains clear and that the casualty's tongue cannot block the throat. All of these procedures are *best taught by experts*.

There are also some excellent videos, such as the 'Save a Life', a guide to emergency aid available from Education and Training Sales, BBC Enterprises Limited (for the address, see page 163.)

The following are some very simple guidelines to help you with some of the day-to-day problems you may encounter. This is however *not* a fully comprehensive list and the advice is very general.

## The A B C of recovery

### A is for Airway
If your child is unconscious, his airway may be narrowed or blocked by his tongue or vomit etc., making breathing difficult or impossible.

- To open the airway, lift the chin and tilt the head backwards (this will extend the head and neck and open the air passage).
- Then push the chin upwards (this will lift the tongue forward and clear the airway). In the open-airway position you should be able to see if anything is still blocking it. Remove any vomit or food, etc. by turning the

head to the side and sweeping the inside of his mouth with your fingers. (See also the section on drowning, opposite).

### B is for Breathing

If your child has stopped breathing, mouth-to-mouth resuscitation is the most efficient way of breathing for him.

- First, open the airway, then either pinch the child's nostrils and put your mouth on his mouth or, if he is very young, cover his nose and mouth with your mouth, *and* blow some air into the child's chest. (The size of the child determines how much air you blow into his chest – with a baby the amount is, of course, very small.)
- Use your cheeks (not your lungs) to puff air in.
- Watch his chest to see if it rises. (If it doesn't rise then the airway may not be fully open and you should readjust the position of the head and jaw and try again.)
- If his chest does rise, then take your mouth away from his and watch his chest fall. Then repeat by blowing air into his lungs in the same way. Then check to see that your child's heart is beating. Do this by placing your fingers (not thumbs) on the pulse at his neck. If you can-

not find a pulse then you will need to use a technique called external chest compression as well as mouth-to-mouth resuscitation to try and start the heart beating again so that it can take the oxygenated blood to the brain.

- For children, mouth-to-mouth resuscitation should be performed at the rate of 20 breaths per minute and it should be continued until breathing returns. (Remember you should only use very gentle puffs for young children.)

### C is for Chest Compression

External chest compression is a technique that is best taught by experts in a practical situation.

The technique must be modified for babies and children and can be dangerous unless it is applied correctly. To learn both this technique and mouth-to-mouth resuscitation, please enrol on a local First Aid course. The guidelines I have given are *very* basic and are *no substitute* for being taught in a practical situation by a trained first aider.

## The recovery position

Following an accident, if your child is unconscious, but breathing, lie him in the position shown opposite before running for help.

The recovery position

This is the position for anyone who has had an accident and is either unconscious or not fully conscious. Of course, the immediate reaction of all parents is to want to hold their child, but the recovery position is one that keeps the airway open and makes sure that the tongue won't block the throat and that any vomit or fluid (e.g., in the case of drowning) can drain away easily. In the case of a suspected spinal injury do not move the casualty unless there is a problem with his airway, breathing or circulation and endeavour to maintain a neutral position (nose, navel and toes all in line).

# Drowning

Pull your child from the water and hold him tilted face down over your arm to help the water drain out of his mouth. Check his breathing and heart beat using the A B C of recovery. If you need to do mouth-to-mouth resuscitation check that his airway is clear first.

Once he is breathing normally, place him in the recovery position, cover him with anything dry to keep him warm and telephone for an ambulance. Remember, it is more important to get oxygen into the lungs than water from the stomach. *Do not waste time.*

Never give up. Countless lives have been saved by people who used mouth-to-mouth resuscitation and external chest compression and refused to abandon hope. Keep going for as long as you are able – you could easily save a life.

## Electric shock

Switch off the power source at once if you can. If not, use any dry non-conductor to pull your child away from the source – a wooden broom will do. If nothing is available, stand on anything that is non-conducting (a newspaper, a rubber mat or a wooden box) and grab your child's loose, dry clothing to pull him away from the source. Follow the A B C of recovery. Treat any burns and take him to hospital unless the shock was very minor. In this case telephone your doctor and take him to the surgery to double-check that all is well.

## Poisoning

Some 30,000 children each year are involved in suspected accidental poisoning either from eating plants or swallowing household or garden chemicals or medicinal products. One survey showed that in nearly three-quarters of the accidents involving medicines, the child was aged between one and two. The peak time for a poisoning incident involving medicines is between 9 and 10 o'clock in the morning. Presumably this is because the medicines are still left out after the morning dose has been taken. Poisoning accidents with household chemicals seem to occur particularly with children about 12 months old, at the crawling or toddling stage, and these, as I'm sure you can guess happen at any time of the day.

Interestingly enough, the survey showed that the safest place to store medicines is in the kitchen and it is the comparatively few medicines in bedrooms or living rooms that are the most likely to be involved in child poisonings. Medicines in the bedrooms are often the central nervous system drugs, for example sedatives and tranquillizers, together with oral contraceptives and painkillers which are frequently stored in lower bedside cabinets that are very readily accessible to children.

If you do keep medicines in the kitchen, don't keep them in the refrigerator as this gives a child easy access to them. Store them in a cupboard well out of reach and preferably in a locked container. All children, especially very young ones, go through a stage when everything goes into their mouth. If you suspect your child has eaten or drunk something that may be poisonous, telephone for an ambulance immediately, try to establish what he has taken and take the empty bottle or container together with any remaining tablets, etc. with you to hospital. Read the outside of the container for any emergency instructions and if there are any, follow them immediately. Some of the symptoms of poisoning are drowsiness, lethargy, vomiting, nausea, dizziness, distress and irritability.

## Suffocation

A baby may suffocate through lying face downwards on a pillow. Do not use a pillow until he is at least two years old — preferably older. Beware of plastic bags that children can put over their heads. Anything that a child can open, climb into and shut the door could cause suffocation.

If your child is suffocating:

- remove the offending article or remove the child to a supply of air (e.g., out of the cupboard)
- if he is conscious and breathing, just comfort him
- if he is unconscious but breathing, place him in the recovery position
- if he has stopped breathing,

open the airway and begin mouth-to-mouth resuscitation and get medical help as soon as you can.

## Choking

Swallowed foreign bodies may cause choking and stop breathing. To remove a foreign body from the airway, it may be necessary to slap four times, high on the shoulder blades and, in extreme cases, to apply an abdominal thrust. This latter technique is best taught by a qualified instructor on a first aid course.

## Burns

Burns and scalds must be cooled as soon as possible for *at least* 10 minutes, if not longer. Put the injured part under *slowly* running cold water or put the burnt legs or arms, etc. into a cold bath until the pain subsides — then apply unmedicated dressings or wet cloths:

- *don't* apply butter, lotions, ointments etc. These will only make the burn worse
- *don't* put on a sticky dressing
- *don't* break any blisters
- *do* seek medical advice for anything other than a very small burn
- watch out for signs of shock.

## Sunburn

A child's skin is much more susceptible to burning than an adult's. Protect his skin with a good high protection factor cream, concentrating especially on the sensitive and most exposed areas. Under the eyes, bridge of the nose, tops of feet and tips of ears always seem to get forgotten and if your child hasn't much hair then make him wear a sun hat. If he does become burnt, make sure he sits somewhere cool and sponge his skin with cool water. Give small sips of cold water. If there is any blistering then you must seek medical advice.

## Fire

If a child's clothing catches on fire, lay him down immediately. This will stop the flames reaching his face. Either put water or anything else non-flammable over him or wrap him tightly in a coat or towel or blanket to smother the flames:

• *don't* use nylon or anything else that could melt to wrap him up with — terrible injuries have resulted from this
• *don't* roll him along the ground, this may make the flames worse.

## Shock

Shock can be caused by extreme physical trauma or by blood or fluid loss. The symptoms are weakness, faintness, sickness or vomiting and the skin may become pale and clammy. Sometimes the patient may start to sweat, breathing becomes shallow and rapid, and it may result in the patient becoming unconscious.

What should I do?

• Comfort the child.
• Lay him down in the recovery position.
• Loosen any tight clothing.
• If his breathing has stopped, use the A B C of recovery.
• Get medical help as soon as possible.
• If possible, raise the lower limbs to divert any surplus blood to vital organs.

# Section 2

## Head injuries — what should I look for?

The skull protects the brain. A bang on the head or a tremendous shaking can result in the delicate tissue hitting the inside of the skull with a bump. The result is concussion.

Concussion can occur without unconsciousness or it may be very fleeting. Even a momentary loss of consciousness should be taken seriously. Lie the child down, treat him for shock and seek medical aid.

Sometimes what seems to be very mild concussion can be very serious, as some of the blood vessels inside the brain may have been damaged and may bleed slowly. You will need to observe your child carefully over the next 24 hours in case he develops any symptoms. These may be severe headaches, pupils of different sizes, impaired speech or balance, vomiting, drowsiness or confused behaviour. If any of these signs develop, call an ambulance.

## Heavy bleeding

If a child cuts himself and, as a result, bleeds copiously you will need to apply pressure directly onto the wound in order to flatten the blood vessels in the area. This will slow down the flow of blood and clots will be able to form. Basically squeeze the sides of the wound together, apply pressure with your thumb and lie the child down. If possible, raise the injured part and support it. Maintain the pressure for between 5 and 15 minutes. This should slow or stop the bleeding. Bandage the wound with a sterile, unused dressing and seek medical help as soon as possible. Sometimes you cannot stop the bleeding by applying direct pressure and you will need to press a pressure point. You will learn more about this if you attend a first aid course.

## Fractured limbs

Try to immobilize the joint above and below the fracture by using the body as a splint — e.g., arm to trunk, good leg to bad leg.

## Hiccups

These should normally only last for a few minutes. If they continue, try putting a paper (not plastic) bag over your child's nose and mouth and let him breathe in and out. This should stop it. If you have no success and the hiccups still persist for more than an hour you should seek medical aid.

## Nosebleeds

This must be one of the commonest problems for growing children. Sit your child down. Ask him to breathe through his mouth and pinch the soft part of his nose or get him to do it.

Get the child to spit out the blood in his mouth and sponge his face and hands. The sight of all the blood is often quite alarming to a child. Release the pressure on his nose after about 10 minutes. If it is still bleeding, repeat for another 10 minutes. Make sure he doesn't rush around once it stops and try to stop him blowing his nose for at least four hours. If the bleeding recurs after 30 minutes seek medical aid.

## Foreign bodies

Some children love to poke objects in their ears and up their noses. Teach them *not* to do this, but if you suspect that this has happened, gently reassure your child and then take him to hospital. Attempting to remove objects yourself is not advisable and you could for example perforate the eardrum.

## Bites

### Animals

If a child is bitten by an animal you must seek medical aid as soon as possible. Animals' mouths contain many germs and their sharp teeth mean that these germs can be injected quite deep into the tissues. Any bite that breaks the skin should be treated quickly to prevent infection. Dog bites should be reported to the police.

Keep your child up to date with his tetanus vaccinations. Tetanus is a horrible and often fatal disease that can easily be prevented by vaccination. After the event may be too late but if he has been vaccinated previously he will probably need a booster if bitten.

If the bite is not deep, wash the wound immediately with soapy water for five minutes. Cover with a sterile, unmedicated dressing and then take your child straight to a doctor.

If the bite is deep, control any serious bleeding, cover the wound and take your child to hospital.

### Snake bites

In England our only poisonous snake is the adder, easily recognized by the V-shaped markings on its back. If you are abroad, however, and your child is bitten by a snake, you should always assume that it is poisonous. Try to remember what it looked like (if you saw it) so that the hospital will know which antidote to use.

If you can, wash the bite out as soon as possible. Otherwise keep your child still and keep the bitten part below the level of the heart. Take him to hospital as quickly as possible.

## Severe allergic reaction

This is also known as anaphylactic shock. It can occur within minutes of an injection of a drug or an insect sting if the child is sensitive to it. Occasionally, it can occur after swallowing something that he is allergic to (e.g., penicillin or a food). The symtoms are:

- signs of shock — he may be cold, clammy, faint, etc.
- probably feeling nauseated
- perhaps difficulty in breathing
- eyes perhaps becoming puffy
- sometimes becoming unconscious.

Call an ambulance immediately and be prepared to resuscitate the child using the A B C of recovery.

In any case, make sure the airway is kept open and put him in the recovery position.

## Hypothermia — what is it?

It can be caused by being in a cold atmosphere (not necessarily below freezing) or by being in cold water for too long or just from not wearing enough clothes in a cold environment.

Babies and small children have greater difficulty in regulating their body temperature than adults. When suffering from hypothermia, they often look very pink and appear very healthy, especially in their feet, hands and face. However, they will soon become limp and very quiet and probably not want any food. It is very important to be aware of this because hypothermia, left unnoticed, can result in death.

In older children it is easier to diagnose in that they will probably complain that they are feeling very cold, their skin will become pale and they will feel very cold to the touch. They may shiver uncontrollably and lose muscle coordination.

If the hypothermia is not advanced, i.e., your child is conscious and his pulse rate is still normal, concentrate on keeping him warm. Take him out of the cold, to shelter and give him warm sweet drinks. *Don't* rub or massage him or tell him to move about to keep warm as this will only encourage further heat loss. One of the best ways of keeping a child warm is to lie him next to your skin and let him take body warmth from you.

If your child is showing signs of unconsciousness or slowed pulse rate you *must* be prepared to use the A B C of recovery and you must take him as quickly as possible to hospital.

*Never give up* even when a pulse cannot be felt. There have been miraculous recoveries after apparent heart stoppage for long periods.

# Section 3

## Losing a tooth

If it is a second tooth, and you can find it, take the tooth with you and find an emergency dentist as quickly as possible. Very occasionally teeth can be saved by prompt action.

## Losing a finger or toe

Control the bleeding using direct pressure and treat for shock. Go at once to hospital. Always take the amputated part with you to hospital as quickly as possible and, if practical, put it in a clean plastic bag or container to protect it.

# Section 4

## What to keep in your first aid kit

Here are a few suggestions that will see you through most of the minor emergencies and could provide you with a useful basis for a kit that you can keep in the kitchen but also take on holiday, in the car or just on a day's outing.

Everyone will want to add their own special requirements to suit their particular family.

- A box of assorted sizes of adhesive dressings, including waterproof ones.
- A packet of sterile gauze useful for cleaning cuts and dressing wounds that are too large for an ordinary dressing.
- A roll of adhesive strapping to hold the gauze in place
- Three packets of medium-sized, one packet of large and one packet of extra large sterile unmedicated dressings.
- Two bandages — one 2.5 cm ( 1

in), one 5 cm (2 in) wide.

- Three triangular bandages in case a temporary sling is needed or to immobilize a fracture.
- A pair of small sharp scissors.
- Safety pins.
- A packet of needles (and matches for sterilizing them) to remove splinters.
- A pair of fine-pointed tweezers to help remove splinters.
- Eyewash and bath.
- Antihistamine cream for insect bites.
- Sun block.

# CHAPTER 7

# AIDS and hepatitis B

We all hope it will never happen to us, that our child won't become infected or become a carrier of either of these two frightening viruses. *BUT it could happen* and to many children it already has. It would be naïve and foolish of us to ignore the threat that these viruses carry.

In this chapter, I want to explain exactly what is safe and what is unsafe behaviour and how to cope should you or your child or one of your or their friends become infectious.

It is much better to recognize the hazards and then learn how to minimize them than to assume that because the risk is low, it is not worth taking some fairly elementary precautions.

## AIDS

### What are HIV and AIDS?

AIDS stands for Acquired Immune Deficiency Syndrome. The virus is generally known as HIV and HIV stands for Human Immuno-deficiency Virus. It attacks the white blood cells and destroys them and prevents the body from making antibodies to fight other diseases.

ARC is an abbreviation for AIDS Related Complex. This condition often strikes HIV positive people and it is one of the first signs of the body's attempt to fight the virus.

# Testing for HIV infection

There are special blood tests that you can have to determine whether or not you are infectious. These are done on a small sample of blood, usually taken from a vein in the arm. The problem with this test is that it cannot tell you for certain that you do not have the virus, since there is a period of time (which varies from person to person) when the virus is effectively 'hiding' and is undetectable. Fortunately, methods of testing are improving all the time.

A *negative* result means that the virus has not been detected. It does not prove that a person is non-infectious. A *positive* result shows that infection with the AIDS virus has occurred and that you are infectious. Since it is important that no mistakes are made on this test, usually the blood is tested twice to make sure that it is positive. If the test is positive then this is what is meant by being HIV antibody positive. *Not everyone who is HIV positive will go on to develop AIDS.*. There are various points of view about this but the general medical opinion is that probably one person in three who is infected will go on to develop AIDS at some stage. Everyone who is tested receives counselling both before and after the test results in order that they may have as much support as is possible.

# Where is the AIDS virus found?

So far the virus has been isolated in:

• blood
• semen
• vaginal mucus
• tears
• saliva
• human milk.

The concentration in tears and saliva is very dilute so the risk of contamination from these is small. In order for infection to take place, there must be a transmission of one of the fluids listed from one person to another.

The number of infected children is at present small, but it is likely to increase. Some children are born to infected mothers: they become infected either during the pregnancy, in utero, or at birth or possibly from breast-feeding. There is a small group of children with haemophilia who have been infected from transfusions of a blood product called factor VIII. Nowadays these blood products, like blood, are tested for the virus, which is then killed by a heat process.

Some estimates indicate that within the next five years there will be over one hundred million people in the world infected with the virus, with approximately one million people with full AIDS. Of course all these figures are reached by extrapolation and no one can really know the extent of the problem, but, even if these figures are only 50 per cent correct (i.e., 50 million infected people) it is still a frightening prospect.

## How else can my child become infected?

The problem is that many people will have no idea that they are infectious and so it is sensible to take some very simple precautions in order to minimize the risks we all take every day.

### Blood brothers
Some children play games that involve becoming 'blood brothers and sisters' with each other. They prick each others thumbs and mix their blood. This should *never* be allowed, nor any other game where body fluids are involved.

### Open wounds
If you or your child has a cut or open wound, it is sensible to cover it. This prevents dirt and dust getting in and also decreases the likelihood of the blood getting on anyone else's skin or vice versa. If one of your child's friends cuts himself it is quite easy for the friend's blood to get onto your child and, if he has an open wound, there is an easy route into your own child's bloodstream. If the friend's blood is infected there is a chance that your child will also become infectious and then the other members of your family will also be at risk.

You may have a group of your child's friends for tea and suddenly one of them develops a violent nosebleed. Your instinct will be to comfort him immediately and you certainly won't think: 'Oh, help, I've got that cut on my finger — I ought to cover it before I help little Johnny.' Of course we would all feel the same, *however,* if you had already covered any cuts there would be no problem and you would have eliminated that small area of risk.

### Toothbrushes
Children (indeed everyone) should have their own toothbrush and, if they use one, their own flannel. This may sound as though I am taking an extreme line here but teeth often bleed when they are brushed. *Toothbrushes and anything that can be contaminated with blood should*

not be shared. Although the problem at present is quite minor in Europe compared to America and Africa, it is escalating. It is *very* important to teach your children safe hygiene practices *now* that will protect them from unnecessary infection, both at present and in the future. This may sound overdramatic but we must start educating ourselves to adopt safe practices and good hygiene habits to reduce any possibility of infection.

Education about AIDS and HIV should start when your child goes to junior school so that he can grow up knowing what is safe behaviour in order to protect himself from exposure to the AIDS virus. Parents, educators and community leaders have a responsibility to provide this information to the young. We should all openly encourage our children to discuss issues about AIDS so that there are no misunderstandings and we can teach them safe habits.

## Artificial insemination

The AIDS virus can be transferred by donating semen. Some cases in Australia have been reported where semen from symptomless carriers of the virus has infected women who were artificially inseminated. The main agencies who specialize in artificial insemination are now screening donors. It is important to ask whether the donor has been screened before agreeing to insemination.

## Travelling abroad

In some of the poorer countries hypodermic needles are sometimes reused without being sterilized properly. So, if you fall ill and need a blood transfusion it is as well to carry one of the AIDS medical kits now on sale. These kits only weigh 112 grams (4 oz) so they can be carried with you everywhere. Remember accidents are more likely to happen at the beach or while travelling than in your hotel room.

The kits contain hypodermic needles, suture materials for stitches, intravenous drip needles and alcohol swabs. The outside of the pack should be clearly labelled with your blood group plus the blood groups of your family and marked 'For medical use only.' Kits are available from MASTA (Medical Advisory Services for Travellers Abroad), the London School of Hygiene and Tropical Medicine or Safa (Safety And First Aid), (see Useful Addresses on page 164 and 165.)

To get the latest health news on your holiday destination contact the Consular Department's travel enquiries unit at the Foreign and Commonwealth Office on 01-270 4129.

## Pierced ears

If your child or teenager wants to have his ears pierced, please make sure it is done by an expert with a non-reusable sterilized needle.

## Sex and drugs

You will notice that I haven't emphasized that, of course, the *main* routes of transmission of the AIDS virus are through sexual acts or from using contaminated needles, for example, for injecting drugs. It is very important to teach your child about these forms of transmission long *before* there is any possibility that they could become involved with such an activity. Many parents simply have no knowledge of what is happening out of school hours (or even within school hours.) It is vital that your sons and daughters have all the knowledge they need in order to be able to say 'no.'

## Symptoms of ARC

Early symptoms are varied but they can include losing weight, fevers, night sweats, skin rashes, diarrhoea, excessive tiredness, loss of appetite, swollen glands in the neck and underarm and having a cough that lasts a long time. Of course, any of these symptoms can be associated with many other infections and no one should jump to a hasty conclusion just because they have got swollen glands, for example.

The virus can then allow serious illnesses to take hold, including pneumonia, cancers, and damage to the brain and central nervous system.

## Some myths dispelled

There have been a great many alarmist articles written about AIDS and how you can catch it. The general medical opinion is that you *cannot* catch AIDS from:

- swimming in swimming pools
- dogs, cats or other domestic animals
- shaking hands
- social kissing
- using the same toilet seat
- sharing cups, cutlery, crockery or towels
- sharing bed linen
- sharing a house, flat or work place with a person with AIDS
- sharing food
- coughing, sneezing and crying
- eating in restaurants

• sharing the communion chalice.

In other words *ordinary social contact is quite safe.*

# Hepatitis

Hepatitis A is common in countries with poor sanitation facilities because the virus is transmitted in human faeces and by contaminated food or drinking water. It can cause sickness, diarrhoea and stomach pains and sometimes jaundice but it is not serious in otherwise healthy people. Usually sufferers recover in a few weeks.

Personal hygiene, especially washing hands before handling food and after using the toilet, will prevent the spread of hepatitis A.

The hepatitis B virus is altogether much more serious. Infected people can become long-term carriers and there is a risk of liver damage. Hepatitis B is *much more infectious* than the AIDS virus, but many of the precautions against AIDS will also protect you against hepatitis B and vice versa.

## Who is at risk?

People returning from countries where hepatitis B is widespread and who have received blood or blood products while they were there, are at risk. In the United Kingdom blood and blood products are screened but it is still possible to receive contaminated blood overseas.

The virus is easily transmitted sexually and drug abusers are also at risk. Health care staff, in particular nurses, doctors, ambulance staff and dentists are especially at risk, as are staff in homes for people with a mental handicap and others in close contact with high-risk patients or clients.

## What are the symptoms of hepatitis B?

These vary from flu-like symptoms with aches, pains and tiredness to sickness, stomach upsets and jaundice (yellow skin). These symptoms can last several weeks and may be followed by a prolonged feeling of exhaustion, which may last up to six months. Some people with hepatitis B may suffer very mild effects or none at all — they may not even realize that they have the virus. The majority of people infected with hepatitis B virus recover completely in about six months and after this time most people are no longer infectious. However, approximately 10 per cent of infected people become *permanently* infectious. They are known as chronic carriers of the virus. Chronic persistent hepatitis B is usually harmless to the carrier, but he is infectious to other people. Chronic active hepatitis B in a small percentage of cases leads to serious liver damage, liver cancer and death.

If you know that you are a hepatitis B carrier or that there is a carrier with whom you or your family have close contact, you must take *every* precaution to prevent any contamination of body fluids. Remember, the hepatitis B virus is *far more infectious* than the AIDS virus. Fortunately there is now a hepatitis B vaccine that is available and your doctor will be able to advise you about this. It is costly but it is available on the NHS to certain groups of people and your family may be eligible. There are many excellent publications and videos giving additional information about AIDS and hepatitis B (see Useful Addresses on pages 163-6.)

---

- Don't let AIDS or hepatitis B become taboo subjects.
- Discuss the problem with your friends.
- Teaching these simple practices *now* may well save your child's life in the future.

# CHAPTER 8

# ANIMALS

Animals and pets can bring a very special new dimension into any child's life. There are, however, several safety issues that are important to consider so that your child can make the most of his pet and also so that you choose an appropriate one for him.

## Diseases from pets and animals

Before any zoonotic (a zoonosis is a disease that can be spread from animals or birds to man) disease can affect a human the animal must first be infected. So, when you are selecting your pet, make sure that you choose only those pets that are fit and healthy. It is sensible to have your animal checked by a vet.

---

### Five basic hygiene rules when dealing with pets

- Choose a pet that is fit and healthy.
- Make sure your pet is up to date with its vaccinations.
- Before touching food, always wash your hands if you've been handling your pet.
- Do not let your pet lick any-one's face.
- Give your pet separate food and water bowls and wash them separately from human dishes.

The common-sense rules of hygiene apply here to avoid any health problems associated with pet animals.

The most common concerns relate to fleas, ringworm, scabies, roundworm and psittacosis. Here are some very simple guidelines but if in doubt, consult your vet.

# Cats

Love your cat and teach your children to treat it with respect. Make sure you follow your vet's advice and your family will have

Give your pet separate food and water bowls and wash them separately from human dishes

many happy years with its pet. This said, it is better to be safe than sorry, so let me warn you of some problems that can occur if cats are neglected or badly handled.

## Bites

There have been some nasty injuries resulting from a cat being mishandled and the cat biting or badly scratching someone. A cat bite may turn septic so ensure that it is carefully cleaned. Cats tend to have a particularly unpleasant range of bacteria as part of their normal mouth flora, which is why care must be taken. You should always seek medical advice if anyone is bitten if they haven't recently had an inoculation against tetanus.

## Parasites

A cat's fur can conceal various parasites, such as fleas, ticks and lice. Gently brushing the fur the wrong way with your hand will often reveal their presence. Look for specks of blackish dirt, usually about the size of a pin head as these are evidence of fleas.

Cat fleas will bite humans if they are displaced from their normal host. Some cat owners become very sensitive to flea bites and a single bite can develop into a painful and highly irritating skin

swelling. And I'm afraid there is more bad news — a single female flea can produce 800 eggs, a pretty frightening thought! The eggs are found on the cat itself, on its bedding and anywhere else that it may have a snooze. So, at the first sign of any fleas, strike with the flea powder or any other method that your vet may recommend.

Your cat may also get round worms or tape worms so make sure that it is regularly wormed. The effects of these worms vary. They can cause diarrhoea, vomiting and may make a cat look potbellied. Usually a kitten is wormed when it is about three weeks old and then at intervals until it is about six months. Subsequently worming twice a year is usually enough.

As far as internal parasites are concerned, the worst, as far as humans are concerned, is the parasite that causes toxoplasmosis. This can occasionally result in causing a pregnant woman to miscarry. So, always wear rubber or plastic gloves when disposing of cat litter. Also, since cats often prefer gardens to cat litter, pregnant lady gardeners are well advised to wear gloves there too.

## A cat and your baby

Never leave a baby alone in the

room with a cat. It may sound as though I'm being over cautious here but your cat may well decide to snuggle up to your child's warm body and could possibly smother him. If your baby is outside in the pram use a cat net to protect him.

## Q fever (a zoonosis)

Q fever is caused by a bacterium that is commonly found in animals and is a typical example of a disease that can spread from animals to humans. The symptoms of Q fever are fever, chills, headache, muscle pain and respiratory symptoms. This disease is most commonly encountered in areas where cows, sheep and goats are kept so, if you live on or near a farm you may be at risk from this.

It is widespread and can be found in both wild and domestic animals. The bacterium is not easily destroyed and can persist for months in clay, sand, wool, skimmed milk, tap water, dried faeces and urine. It is most commonly spread by simply being in the air but can also be transmitted through milk. In one case an

Pregnant lady gardeners are well advised to wear gloves

infected domestic cat resulted in 13 cases of Q fever amongst a group of extended family and friends. Fortunately its spread to humans is uncommon.

Typically this illness lasts from 5 to 14 days and the patient responds to suitable medical treatment. At the moment, however, there is no acceptable vaccine.

The likelihood of your pet harbouring Q fever, or indeed, many other bacteria, etc., will be greatly reduced if it is kept in clean surroundings, groomed frequently and its litter is changed regularly.

## Kittens and scratching

Certain traits exhibited in young kittens can become quite serious problems when the cat is older if they are not corrected while they are still kittens. Some kittens scratch and bite when they are being played with. If yours does this, pick it up and put it in another part of the room, then ignore it. If all else fails then a quick spray of cold water is a fairly effective deterrent.

## Playthings

Don't let your child's playthings become intermixed with your cat's or those of any other pets. A cat's toys will be covered with its own bacteria and will be highly unsuitable for a child. The most difficult time will be when your baby is crawling and going through the stage when everything seems to go in its mouth. Take great care.

## Introducing a new cat to the household

You will need to be careful about this. Children are so enthusiastic and inquisitive that they will tend to overpower a new kitten. If your children are not used to cats then explain to them how they can help look after it, but don't let them pick up the cat till both parties have become well used to each other.

Dogs are usually reasonably tolerant towards a new kitten, but if there are already other cats in the household, take it very gently. Keep the cats well apart and only very gradually introduce them to each other.

# Dogs

Much of the above information also applies to dogs and puppies.

Here again, follow my basic hygiene guidelines and make

sure that you keep fleas, worms, ringworm, ticks, etc. well under control.

Any new (uncaged) pet should be introduced into a household gently and the children should be shown how to treat it. Animals don't like being taken by surprise so make sure your mischievous seven-year-old doesn't decide to tease your dog. Many dogs are exceptionally patient and will put up with all sorts of children's games, but there does come a point when even the most placid animal may start to become agitated. This is when accidents can happen. Teach your children to love and respect their pet and this way you will minimize the risk.

## Caution

Don't forget that worming medicines are poisons and should be used and stored very carefully.

Although most worms that can live in a dog will not cause any harm to a human there are two varieties that you should be aware of:

- **Echinococcus**
  This is a tiny tapeworm that is too small to be seen by the naked eye. Like every other tapeworm the eggs are passed out with the dogs faeces. If a

human swallows the worm's eggs (you can get them on your hand by stroking an infected dog) then a cyst may develop in the lungs or liver and cause a very serious illness. Fortunately this is very rare but it does show how very important it is to prac-tise good hygiene with pets.

- **Round worms**
  Here again, the eggs of this worm are passed out by the dog and they can't be seen by the naked eye. If a small child swallows the eggs the larvae will hatch and get into the blood stream. Most of these will die but some may continue to live and these can arrive in the brain or the back of the eye and can sometimes result in blindness. This, I stress, is very rare. If you keep your pets free of round worm and insist on handwash-ing you will prevent most prob-lems. In any case it is sensible to worm your dog every six months to keep troubles to a minimum.

Make sure that your dog has all its vaccinations so that it is as fit and healthy as possible. In many countries it is a requirement for a dog to be vaccinated against rabies at regular intervals. Britain has so far managed to keep the disease out of the country and your dog will only need the vaccine if it is going to travel abroad.

## Dog bites

At least 50,000 children in England and Wales attend accident and emergency departments of hospitals annually because they have either been bitten or stung. The worst ages for being bitten by a dog seem to be between two and three and between seven and nine years old. Strangely, many more boys get bitten than girls! For this age group, bites are usually the result of the child taunting or sometimes molesting the dog. Babies are usually bitten if the animal is jealous of the presence of the child. In most cases the dog involved is known to the child.

## Jealousy

Remember that a dog is a pack animal and, even if he is the only dog in the household, he still will need to establish his family. A new human baby may well cause your dog to become jealous and he may feel that his place in the pack has become dislodged. Don't leave the baby alone in the room with your dog until you are absolutely sure that your pet has accepted the baby as part of the family and that he is not seen by the dog as a threat or a rival for attention.

## The law

The Animals Act, 1971, makes you responsible for damage caused by your animal (and in law any animal owned by a child is automatically the responsibility of his parents). So, for example, if the family labrador roams freely on the road and is hit by a car, you may well be liable for the damage caused to the car and any injury to the driver and the passengers. Also, if your child's dog kills or maims sheep or poultry on the local farm you will be held responsible. A farmer may also be within his rights if he shoots your pet if it is on his land and worrying his livestock.

# Furry things in cages

By 'furry things' I mean rabbits, hamsters, gerbils, guinea pigs and mice. Like all animals these may be prone to fleas, mites, worms, etc., and it is important to check them regularly.

The organism that causes *Pneumocystis carinii* (a rare form of pneumonia) was discovered in 1910 in guinea pigs by a Brazilian scientist, Dr Carini. Fortunately it is one of tens of thousands of organisms that are held in check by normal people's immune systems. However, if you have a very sick member of the household (someone suffering from post-viral syndrome, for example, or, worse still, someone who has AIDS) then you must take extra care.

There are a number of other pets that you might perhaps have considered, such as an exotic squirrel or a monkey or chinchilla, but these are rather a specialist group and you should take specific advice from your vet before considering buying them. However, a quick word about monkeys. It is almost impossible to house-train a monkey. Male monkeys sometimes can be remarkably accurate with their aim and you may end up feeling very wet and unsavoury. Also monkeys bite — at any time. Need I say more?

## Fish

Fish do suffer from fungal infections, so, if your children put their hands into the fish tank, make sure they wash them afterwards. Be particularly careful of any goldfish that you may win at a fair. Perhaps I've had bad luck, but every time I've brought a goldfish home it has caused fungal infections to the others in the tank.

## Deer

If you are lucky enough to live near a park or visit one there may be herds of wild deer there. Often these are quite tame as they are used to humans, but you should tell your children to be very careful, as, particularly during the rutting season, they can become very aggressive and can cause quite severe injuries.

Feeding the fawns is particularly dangerous. It is much better to tell your child just to look but not go too close to any wild animals. Many years ago when I was visiting the New Forest in Hampshire we came across a little girl whose face was covered in blood. She had stood too close to one of the wild ponies and it had kicked backwards and badly injured her. Wild animals are not used to humans so keep your children a safe distance away.

Deer can become quite aggressive in the rutting season

# Horses

## Harsh facts

- Between 10,000 and 15,000 children attend accident and emergency departments in England and Wales every year as a result of accidents while horse riding.
- Of these accidents, 45 per cent are caused by falls.
- Horse kicks are the cause of 33 per cent of them.
- Crushing causes 7 per cent of them.

If your child wants to ride a horse, make sure he wears a proper hard hat (BS 6473) and suitable clothes, especially shoes. Check also that his riding school treats road safety as a priority. The British Horse Society has a riding and road safety certificate that everyone who is going to learn to ride should study.

Occasionally horses butt and bite children and can even step on their feet. The main reasons for these accidents are:

- inexperienced riders
- the horse is startled
- the horse is the wrong size for its rider
- the riding hat does not conform with BS 6473 or it did not fit properly or it is not fastened.

## Some simple safety points

- Make sure your child is taught to ride by an experienced riding instructor.
- Inexperienced riders should never be allowed on the road without being accompanied by an experienced person.
- Children should understand the Highway Code and apply the three C's when riding:
  Care
  Courtesy
  Consideration
- All pony tack should be correctly fitted with stirrups the right size and length and in good repair.
- Shoes should have hard soles and heels.
- Reflective clothing for your child and leg bands for the horse should be used if he is riding after lighting-up time. Safety lamps should also be worn on the stirrups.

# Birds — caged and otherwise

## Wild birds

Many birds — especially pigeons in cities do spread diseases through the various organisms that are found in their droppings. One in particular is known as cryptococcus, which, although it will not normally cause any problems could be dangerous to someone with a weakened immune system.

## Caged birds

Ornithosis, otherwise known as psittacosis, is almost the only infection that can be transmitted by birds to humans. Imported parrots are probably the biggest danger but now imported birds have to undergo 35 days quarantine, which does reduce the risk.

## Allergies

Some children (and adults) can react quite badly to feathers and fur. They can trigger a number of asthma or allergic responses including rashes, itchy eyes and streaming noses.

Please don't think that this chapter is designed to put you off owning a pet. Many pets are wonderful companions and can teach a child to care for and respect other animals. They bring a great deal of happiness to many many families. But, please, take care, choose carefully, teach your family the simple rules of hygiene and treat your pets with the respect they deserve.

# CHAPTER 9

# CHILD ABUSE

## Harsh facts

- A recent MORI survey estimated that one in ten British adults had at least one sexually abusive experience in childhood.
- Of the reported cases in Britain of child sexual abuse, 75 per cent were committed by a person *known* to the child.
- Both boys and girls are at risk.

I pondered long and hard as to what exactly I should call this chapter — molestation, sexual abuse, keeping safe from adults ...? None of these titles really conveys the myriad situations that a child can find himself in and where it is vital that he knows what to do to keep himself safe from other people.

Time and time again I have found that safety is very largely a question of always being at least one or more steps ahead of the game. For example, a situation is not really so alarming if you have already discussed the possibility that such and such an event or disaster might happen and you have calmly worked out what you would or should do to minimize the dangers. Similarly, if you have already put yourself hypothetically in this situation you may also be able to work out how to avoid getting there in the first place. All the way through this book you will have seen this approach put into action. Think about 'fire'. First, we worked out how to avoid it and then we discussed what we would do if disaster struck and we were faced with a fire ourselves.

Let's think about the sort of difficult or unpleasant situations our child could be faced with and then I will show you some simple guidelines that have been worked out by a superb organization called 'Kidscape' to show our children how to react.

---

## Difficult situations

- A bully at school, in the playground or park teases your child.
- At the swimming pool an older child tries to touch your child when he is changing.
- Someone tries to bribe your child to do something he doesn't want to do.
- A flasher accosts your child.
- A stranger comes to collect your child from school and says that you have asked him to do this as your car has broken down.
- A stranger follows your child home and starts to talk to him.
- The phone rings — your child answers it and it turns out to be an obscene caller.
- Someone your child knows touches him in a way that makes him feel uncomfortable.
- Your son is out for a bike ride and a group of boys jump out from the bushes and push him over.

---

No one could write about child abuse without mentioning a very special person called Michele Elliot. Michele is an educational psychologist, a teacher and a mother of two. In 1986 she founded the organization, Kidscape (see page 164 for their address).

Kidscape offers training courses, particularly for schools, teachers and social workers, and has also produced a number of special programmes to help parents and teachers show children how to keep themselves safe. Michele has also written a number of excellent books, both for children and adults, and there is also a very good Kidscape video.

The educational material from Kidscape is fun — my children have read *The Willow Street Kids*, (Michele's book for children, published by Andre Deutsch, 1986) at least three times (twice with me and once on their own) and the guidelines are really very simple and extremely effective. Kidscape has kindly allowed me to reproduce their excellent Kidscape Keep Safe Code and the golden rules for Good Sense Defence.

## The Kidscape keep safe code

- **Hugs**
  Hugs and kisses are nice, especially from people we like. Even hugs and kisses that feel good and that you like should never be kept secret.

- **Body**
  Your body belongs to you and not to anyone else. This means *all* of your body, particularly the private parts covered by your swim suit. If anyone ever tries to touch your body in a way that confuses or frightens you, say 'No' and tell.

- **No**
  If anyone older than you, even someone you know, tries to kiss or touch you in a way you don't like or that confuses you, or which they say is supposed to be a secret, say 'No' in a very loud voice. Don't talk to anyone you don't know when you are alone or just with other children. You don't have to be rude, just pretend you didn't hear and keep on walking.

- **Run**
  If a stranger, a bully or even someone you know tries to harm you or touch you in a frightening way, run away and get help. Make sure you always run towards other people or to a shop, if you can.

- **Yell**
  Wherever you are, it is all right to yell if someone is trying to hurt you. Practice yelling as loud as you can in a big, deep voice by taking a deep breath and letting the yell come from your stomach, not from your throat.

- **Tell**
  Tell a grown-up you trust if anyone frightens you or tries to touch you in a way that makes you feel unsafe. It is never your fault if an older person does this. If the first grown-up doesn't believe you, keep telling until someone does. It might not be easy, but even if something has already happened that you have never told before, try to tell now. Who could you tell?

- **Secrets**
  Secrets such as surprise birthday parties are fun, but some secrets are not good and should never be kept. No older person should ever ask you to keep a kiss, hug or touch secret. If anyone does, even if you know that person, tell a grown-up you trust.
- **Bribes**
  Don't accept money or sweets or a gift from anyone without first checking with your parents. Most of the time it will be all right, like when you get a present for your birthday from your grandma. But some people try to trick children into doing something by giving them sweets or money. This is called a bribe; don't ever take one!
- **Code**
  Have a code word or sign with your parents or guardians, that only you and they know. If they need to send someone to collect you, they can give that person the code. Don't tell the code to anyone else.

© Kidscape 1986

Having a code word is a brilliant idea. Work out your code with your children now.

## Kidscape extra

- Don't answer the door if you are at home on your own.
- Don't tell anyone over the telephone that you are at home alone. Say that your Mum will ring back, she's in the bath — or any other excuse you can think of.
- Always tell your parents or whoever is taking care of you where you are going and how you can be contacted.
- If you get lost, go to a shop or a place with lots of people and ask for help, or find a policeman or policewoman to ask.
- Travel in a carriage or train where there are other people.
- When you're out on your own, keep far enough away from people you don't know so that you can't be grabbed and could run away.
- Never play in dark or deserted places.
- Carry enough money for your return trip home and never spend it on anything else.
- Memorize your telephone number and address.

Bribes: don't accept sweets from strangers

- Know how to contact your parents or a neighbour.
- If you have no money, but need to ring home in an emergency, dial 100 and ask the operator to place a reverse charge call.
- Learn how to make an emergency telephone call:
  - dial 999 and the operator will say, 'Emergency, what is your number?'
- give the telephone number you are speaking from
- the operator asks, 'which service do you want?' and you say 'Police'.
- the operator puts you through to the police who will ask you for the telephone number again, your name and where you are, so that they can find you. Then you tell them what's wrong.

This sounds like it would take a long time, but it usually happens very quickly. Always get an adult to make an emergency telephone call, if possible. No one should ever make one unless there is a real emergency.

Kidscape also produces a lovely poster for your child to colour and fill in. One part of the poster is an outline of a person and the child is asked to 'colour in green where you like to be touched'. Matthew (my six-year-old) decided that he specially liked being touched in his arm pits, on his knees and on the soles of his feet and I never knew that until then!

## What you can do to help your child

- Don't give your child T-shirts or school satchels with his name printed boldly on them. It is all too easy for a stranger to walk up and greet him by his name. 'Hello, Tom' may lull Tom into a false sense of security.
- Play 'What if ?' games. Imagine with your child some of the situations we discussed at the beginning of this chapter and work out together what the best way would be to handle them. Practice yelling, and saying no, and running away as fast as you can.
- Role play. We have terrific fun in my family when we do this — the children love it and, because we've previously discussed how to react, it's never frightening and they are always proud of knowing how to cope.
- Spend time talking to your children, encouraging them to tell you if anything is worrying them. Don't be too busy to listen.
- Talk about good secrets and bad secrets and explain that bad secrets shouldn't be kept. If someone has a bad secret they should find an adult they can trust and tell them. If that adult doesn't listen then they must find another and must make sure that they keep going until someone does listen.
- Always make sure that you use a reliable babysitter. Check with the children and ask them questions about any games they played with them.
- Watch out for danger signals — a change in a child's behaviour, a sudden lack of concentration or regression to more babyish habits. Often a disturbed or worried child will start thumb-sucking, bed-wetting or needing

a blanket, like Linus. He may burst into tears for no reason or be nervous about going to a friend's or relative's house.

- In older children, particularly girls, eating disorders such as anorexia (nervosa or bulimia) can sometimes be an indication of sexual abuse.

Be aware. Listen and talk. Don't dismiss any niggling doubts you may have. You, as the child's parent, will know your child better than anyone else. If *you* don't pick up the warning signals, perhaps no one else will.

Don't give your child T-shirts with his name printed in large letters on them

# What to do if you suspect your child has been abused

You will probably feel considerably shaken and will need to get advice. There are a number of excellent organizations that will help and these are listed under Useful Addresses on pages 163-6.

You can also contact your doctor or your church and, in some cases, you may need to contact the police or the social services department.

# Cruelty and the law

It is a criminal offence for anyone over the age of 16 who is in charge of a child to be cruel to that child (The Children's and Young Person's Act.) Cruelty in this context can mean neglect or exposure to unnecessary suffering. If you leave a small child in a car, for example, this could, in certain cases, be construed as exposing him to unnecessary suffering. Cruelty can also mean brutality.

Sometimes a child is taken into care. This may happen if he is under the age of 17. An application for a care order may be brought by a local authority, social services department, a local educational authority, a police officer or an officer of an authorized society, such as the NSPCC.

An Order may only be made if the applicant can prove that:

- the child is being ill treated
- or that the child's proper development is being avoidably prevented or his health is being avoidably impaired or neglected
- or it is probable that the above condition will occur because a court has found that another child of the same household has been neglected or ill-treated
- or because a person in the same household as the child has been convicted of a serious offence against a child or children
- or the child is exposed to moral danger
- or the child is beyond the control of his parent or guardian
- or the child is not receiving suitable efficient full-time education.

Care orders are not issued lightly

and it will only be when a number of other measures have failed that the local authority will decide that they must take the child into safer surroundings.

The local authority is the organization that has the responsibility to make inquiries into any such incidents. However, anyone — neighbour, friend or relative — can and should report any situation where they suspect that a child is being ill-treated in any way. If you are worried about a child and are not able to do anything directly, you must tell someone in authority who will be able to help. It is certainly not an easy thing to do, but who could live with the knowledge that they could have saved a child's life if only they had had the courage to speak up?

# Teenagers

Here, again, many of the Kidscape guidelines are very important. When I was new to London, I was on a crowded tube train: a man behind me started touching my legs. I yelled 'Stop bothering me'! He was so surprised, he quickly moved away and the rest of my journey was completely uneventful!

We all remember with horror the dreadful story of Suzy Lamplugh, the pretty estate agent who went out for an appointment with the now infamous 'Mr Kipper' to show him round a house and was never seen again. Suzy's mother, Diana, has set up the Suzy Lamplugh Trust, which works to inform women how to defend themselves in the workplace. Although the advice that the Trust gives is geared towards women at work, we should be teaching our older children *now* so that when they do leave school they are not so vulnerable. Two situations upon which the Trust has already given advice are 'jogging' and 'mini-cabbing' and I am extremely grateful to Diana Lamplugh for her permission to reproduce the Trust's guidelines here:

## Jogging

- Try to run in company — two (or more) pairs of eyes are always better than one.
- Tell somebody where you're going running and how long you're likely to be.
- Wear clothes in which you feel confident and unprovocative. Make sure you can be seen at

Try to run in company

night — light-coloured gear and reflective bands or stickers are important. Don't wear jewellery.

- If the street is deserted, run down the middle of the pavement, not near bushes, doorways, etc.
- Run facing oncoming traffic to see what's coming.
- Avoid kerb crawlers, and don't stop to give a driver directions, however innocent the enquiry seems.
- *Never* take short cuts!
- Keep to busy, well-lit and well-populated streets, especially if you are running alone.
- Vary your route and your times — any routine can easily be observed.
- Be aware of your surroundings and of where you could go for help.
- If it makes you feel more confident, run with a personal attack alarm in your hand or a whistle.
- If you think you're being followed, cross the road and keep running. Then, if your pursuer continues to follow you, make for a busy area or well-lit house to ask for help.

- Don't exhaust yourself entirely, and make sure you're not too tired to defend yourself.
- Leave a light on outside the house as you will be most vulnerable on your return. Have your key ready to get in quickly and make sure no one follows you in.
- Some women take their dogs out running, and this may help your confidence, especially if your dog is large and ferocious looking.
- Don't wear personal stereo headphones — you will not be able to hear a would-be attacker.

## Mini-cabbing

- Before you leave your home or place of work to go out for the evening, make sure you have with you the telephone number of a reputable mini-cab company. Just in case you miss the last bus or a promised lift, you know that you will still get home safely.
- When you book your mini-cab, ask the company for the name of the driver they are sending. When he arrives to collect you, ask him to tell you his name and the name of his mini-cab company, to check that he really is the man sent for the job.
- Get in the back of the cab.

- Try to share a cab with a friend — it's cheaper and safer.
- Although it's natural to chat with your driver, don't give away any information about your personal habits — where you work, who you live with, etc.
- If your driver is taking an unusual route to your destination, or even travelling in the wrong direction, tactfully suggest a short cut to get you there.
- If you feel very uncomfortable with your driver, ask him to stop and drop you off in a well-lit, busy place with which you are familiar, where you can go for safety.
- If your destination is your home, ask the driver to drop you a couple of doors away from it — he doesn't need to know your exact address.
- When you arrive at your destination, have cash ready to pay the driver. Get out of the car as soon as you arrive, and then pay the driver through his window.
- Have your front door keys ready in your pocket and enter your home as quickly as possible.
- Before you use any mini-cab company whose car or number you may have, check that they are the type of respectable firm that you are happy to use. Ask

your friends if they know of them, check they're listed in the telephone directory or even go to see what their offices look like, if possible.

- Think ahead about how you would protect yourself in the exceptional instance of harassment, robbery or assault.

- If anything happens that makes you feel uncomfortable, get the driver's name and registration number and report it to his mini-cab company. Should the worst happen, go to the police.

- Remember, most mini-cab drivers are reliable and honest. The last thing on their mind is trying to harm you, they simply want to provide you with a good service and a safe journey to your destination.

By now you will have read the chapter in this book on AIDS. In it you read that it is estimated that within the next five years there will be millions of people infected with the AIDS virus — and these people will not all be in Africa and the United States. It looks as though it will become a very major problem for us all.

One of my great fears is that, as a result, we will see a very substantial increase in the number of cases of rape *and* of sexual/child abuse because some HIV carriers will become so lonely and desperate. Unfortunately there may be some for whom the burden is too great — rejected by friends and former lovers they may seek other furtive avenues with appalling results.

Educate your teenage children, contact organizations such as Kidscape and the Suzy Lamplugh Trust and encourage your children to enrol for self-defence classes. There are some very simple techniques using hands, fingers, feet, knees and elbows that can be most effective. Above all, teach your child calmly and positively. Fear produces irrational behaviour: education and discussion will help give your child the *confidence* he needs to cope with a difficult situation and the ability to *avoid* many of the dangers.

# Drug abuse

I have included a short section on drug abuse in this chapter since it seems to me that people who encourage children to try any sort of drug are abusing that child. They — the 'pushers' — are quite clearly child abusers.

Let's hope that none of us ever

has to handle the problem of having a child who is a drug abuser. However, the majority of adolescent drug takers are usually just experimenting. If you can spot the signs early enough and get help, you may prevent what started off as a silly game becoming a serious, even life-threatening problem.

If there is one central message that I want to get across in this book, it is that safety is about being wise *before* the event. By being aware of, and thinking about, the dar̃ers, we can protect our children. Drug abuse is an excellent example of this. If we assume that it won't happen to *our* children, we may not find out until it is too late.

## Why use drugs?

For many youngsters, drug and solvent abuse seems an easy solution for coping with self-consciousness, loneliness, lack of confidence, school exams, unhappiness and all the other problems associated with growing up. Sometimes drugs will be used in order to challenge parental authority and others will use drugs just to be accepted by their peers. What they use will depend on what is available. There are many excellent organizations that will give information, advice and even anonymous help and counselling (see pages 163-6 for addresses).

In this section I have concentrated on solvent abuse and this is followed by some general information and key points to look out for that may help you identify a problem in its early stages.

There are five major types of drugs:

- volatile solvents, such as adhesives, glue and aerosols
- sedatives and tranquillizers, including alcohol, barbiturates and minor tranquillizers
- stimulants, such as caffeine, tobacco, amphetamines, cocaine and crack
- opiates, which are derivatives of the opium poppy, such as heroin and morphine. There are also some synthetic derivatives such as codeine, DF 118 and distalgesic
- hallucinogenic drugs, such as LSD, cannabis and psilocybin (hallucinogenic fungi).

## Solvent abuse

### Harsh facts

- In 1986, two children died every week in the United Kingdom from the effects of solvent sniffing.

No one knows the real extent of the problem, but one estimate is that about 10 per cent of youngsters have tried solvent sniffing. Many children are just experimenting and it is often only a passing phase, but some become regular users and quite often sniff in groups. Sadly, some young children are just copying their older brothers and sisters.

## Which substances are most commonly used?
Some of the most commonly abused products are:

- solvent-based adhesives and glues
- aerosols
- petrol
- typewriter correction fluid
- nail varnish
- nail varnish remover
- dry cleaning fluids
- lighter fuel
- solvent-based marker pens
- shoe and metal polish.

There are many more substances that could be added to this list. All of these products contain volatile hydrocarbons that, when inhaled or 'sniffed' produce an effect very similar to alcohol or anaesthetics. The effect is very swift, but wears off quickly once the inhalation stops.

Solvent sniffing can cause:

- loss of control
- slurred speech
- loss of consciousness
- hallucinations

As with any drug there is an increased chance of an accident after sniffing. Some drownings and road accidents have been associated with solvent abuse. Sometimes sniffers use plastic bags to cover their faces and, if they become unconscious, they can suffocate. Others have died from choking on their own vomit. If an aerosol is sprayed straight into the mouth, it may cause the tissues of the mouth and throat to swell and to produce sticky mucus. The airways can block and cause asphyxiation. It is also very dangerous to play sport or go running immediately after sniffing aerosols — there is a risk of 'sudden sniffing death' due to heart failure.

## What are the signs to look for?
The short-term effects are:
- flushed skin
- bloodshot eyes
- dilated pupils
- vomiting

The longer term effects are:
- a rash on the face (especially around the nose and mouth)
- irritability
- tiredness

- a runny nose
- poor memory
- lack of co-ordination

Other indications are to be found by looking, listening and smelling.

- *look* — you may notice any of these above signs or you may find some of your solvent-based products are missing
- *listen* — you may notice slurred or incoherent speech
- *smell* — often the smell of the solvent clings to a person's clothing and his breath smells.

**Who can you go to for help?**
Your family doctor can give medical advice and support or he may refer you to a specialist organization.

Your child's school teachers can be helpful. If the problem is occurring at school, it is important that the staff know so that they can take immediate action. They can also call in experts who are trained in explaining the very serious dangers of sniffing to children as part of a health education programme.

You can also contact the police. Sniffing is not illegal but the police will be able to provide advice and tell you where best to go for further help.

There are a number of local and national organizations that specialize in giving advice and support to the families of drug and solvent abusers and to the users themselves. Don't be afraid to telephone them — they are there to help.

## Sedatives and tranquillizers

Barbiturates such as phenobarbitone are often referred to as barbs, downers or sleepers. In small doses they produce a similar effect to a couple of alcoholic drinks (relaxation and reduction of anxiety.) Larger doses will either induce sleep or cause a drunken-like state with slurred speech and a lack of coordination. Higher doses still can cause blackouts, aggressive behaviour, unconsciousness and even death.

Minor tranquillizers mainly include the benzodiazepines such as Valium, Librium, Ativan and Mogadon. In small doses they produce a feeling of well-being and a loss of inhibition. The side-effects can be drowsiness, lethargy, disorientation and confusion.

Alcohol produces many of the effects described above. In excess it can cause liver damage, gastric irritation and even brain damage. Teach, by example and NEVER drink and drive.

## Stimulants

As the name suggests, these stimulate the central nervous system.

The effects of amphetamines are to give a feeling of alertness and lots of energy, reduce the appetite, increase heart rate, dilate the pupils and generally produce a restless excited state. Very often stimulant users become very talkative and over-enthusiastic. Larger doses can cause panic states and paranoid delusions. Sometimes users suffer from slight tremors.

Cocaine has similar effects to those of amphetamines. Its after-effects can include tiredness, insomnia and depression. One of the other problems is that cocaine is often adulterated with other harmful substances.

Antidepressants such as Tofranil and Nardil have unpleasant side-effects such as blurred vision, dry mouth, etc., so they are not commonly abused. They can dramatically increase the physical effects of amphetamines and can cause very severe reactions that can lead to death.

## Opiates

These produce five main effects:

• pain relief

• mood change — often euphoria and a tendency to withdraw
• vomiting
• pinpoint pupils
• constipation.

One of the major long-term effects is the marked social withdrawal and physical self-neglect that results from using these drugs. There are also associated illnesses from infections caused by unsterile techniques of regular injectors.

Girls who take opiates often have very irregular menstrual cycles which may even stop for many months.

## Hallucinogenic drugs

LSD is usually taken orally. Users often appear restless, agitated and excited, they may suffer from nausea or tremors, they may sweat and have poor coordination. Often someone under the influence of LSD will be very frightened or suspicious, he may be aggressive and self-destructive and may think he is going mad.

To control a person in this state you must reassure him, talk quietly and make sure he is in a peaceful place away from loud music and noises that will only frighten him more. The effects may last as long as 8-10 hours.

There are several types of fungi

containing chemicals that have a similar effect on the brain as LSD. 'Magic Mushrooms', for example, contain the chemical psilocybin. Many of these fungi are very dangerous as most of them contain the poison muscarine.

Cannabis has the short-term effect of exaggerating the person's mood and heightening his sensory perceptions. It can make a person very forgetful and can sometimes cause panic reactions. Heavy cannabis use can lead to self-neglect and apathy.

If your child or teenager starts showing marked changes in behaviour and mood or perhaps some of the physical signs that I have highlighted, you may be able to arrest what could become a life threatening problem before it really takes hold.

Don't think:

• it couldn't happen to my child, it could.

Be wise *before* the event.

Unless parents, carers and educators all take a very positive role, the number of drug and solvent abusers will continue to increase. We must not let that happen.

# CHAPTER 10

# TRANSPORT

Statistically you or someone in your family will be killed or injured in a road accident. Follow this chapter's advice and help reverse the trend.

---

## Harsh facts

- In 1986, 41,000 children (under 15) in Great Britain were injured as result of a road accident.
- Of these 17 per cent were under five years old and 35 per cent were aged between five and nine years.

---

What is so shocking is that so many road tragedies could have been prevented. Human error is the major factor in almost every road accident.

We must all teach our children so well that good habits become second nature and bad habits are not allowed to develop. In so doing I believe that, not only will we create safer pedestrians and passengers, we will produce safer and more considerate drivers for the future.

## In the car

### Seat belts

Over 50 children are killed and over 7,000 injured while travelling unrestrained in the backs of cars each year.

The Department of Transport

reports that child restraints can reduce the risk of death by about three quarters and *rear seat belts halve the risk for adults*. Also, people in the front are often killed or maimed by people travelling in the back unrestrained. So, when both front and rear passenger seats are being used, ideally the lighter passengers should sit in the back and you should certainly encourage any back seat passenger to wear a seat belt.

The law that came into force on the 31st January 1983 requires anyone travelling in the front seat of a car to wear an approved seat belt (one that bears either a kitemark or one of the European marks).

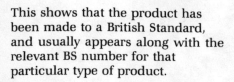

BSI Kitemark

This shows that the product has been made to a British Standard, and usually appears along with the relevant BS number for that particular type of product.

European approval symbols

Loose objects in a car are thrown around in an accident. Don't let your children be those loose objects — they could be seriously hurt or killed. Over 1,000 children are killed or seriously injured each year like this.

## For children up to 12 months old

You can use either a rearward-facing safety seat (BS AU202, ECE Reg 44) that is held in place by an adult seat belt, or a carrycot restrained with straps made to BS AU186:1983.

The rearward-facing safety seat can be used in either the front or back seat. If you use a carrycot, put your baby in it with his head *away* from the sides of the car and make sure you use a cot cover or something similar to prevent your baby being thrown out in the event of a crash.

## For children aged between nine months and four years

Use an approved car safety seat (BS 3254). These car seats raise the child off the ordinary back seat and then he can see out of the window and is much more content (see page 148).

## For older children

Over the age of four a child may wear a child harness BS 3254 or an adult seat belt used with a special

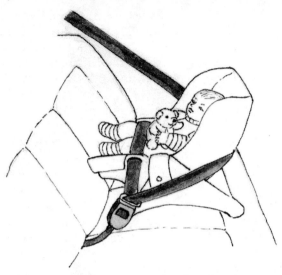

Special rearward-facing safety seats can be fitted utilizing an adult seat belt (use for babies up to 10 kg/22 lb)

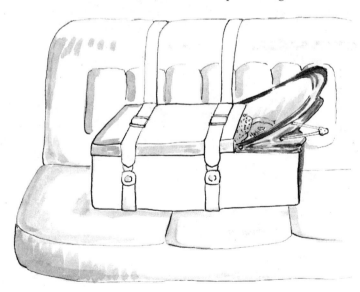

Rigid carrycots can be placed in special restraint straps. The buckle, quick-release version is safest (use for babies up to 10 kg/22 lb)

Child car seats (use for children up to 18 kg/40 lb)

Child harness

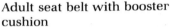
Adult seat belt with booster cushion

Don't make do with adult seat belts for children. They can be very uncomfortable for them and dangerous.

booster cushion BS AU185:1983 to help the belt fit properly. He could also use a lap and diagonal seat belt, which is adjustable.

## Travelling in a car

Teach your child not to play with door handles or window handles (it is often easy to mistake one for the other) and it is sensible to lock the back doors whenever you go out in the car. Some cars have child locks fitted on the back doors: even so, teach them *never* to play with the handles. It may not always be your car they are travelling in and not all cars have child locks! What else can you do to make the time you spend in your car safer?

### Skid pans

Could you cope if your car went into a skid on black ice? I had terrific fun recently driving on our local skid pan, learning what to do. There are quite a number of these up and down the country and they all run good courses that teach you how to cope with wet, slippery or icy driving conditions.

Most skid pans have special cars that you can use if you would rather not risk using your own, and most offer theoretical as well as practical instruction. When I did my course, I was told that half an hour on a skid pan was worth five years' driving experience — and I can well believe it. (Ring your local council offices for more information.)

**Regular checks**

Check your car regularly to make sure that brakes, seat belts, lights, tyres, windscreen wipers and horn are all in working order. Be very careful about what you store on your back seat — particularly what is stored on the shelf by the back window. I cringe when I drive past cars with bottles or heavy road maps on these shelves; one sharp push on the brakes will turn your road map into a weapon that will be as effective as a karate chop on the child in the back seat.

All cars should have a well-equipped first aid kit, together with a fire extinguisher (a BCF extinguisher is suitable), securely fitted: teach your children never to play with them.

Here is a check-list of reminders when transporting children:

---

## Remember

- Always walk round the back of your car before reversing out of your drive. Small children and animals are often out of your rear vision. Make sure your exit route is clear.
- Children should use the door nearest to the pavement when getting in or out of a car.
- When opening the door make sure it can open safely without hitting people, objects or following cars.
- Make sure all doors are closed properly and locked.
- Make sure children in the back seats wear seat belts even on the shortest trips.
- Check your rear mirror vision.
- Check your rear window shelf.
- Make it a rule that no child may touch the door or window handle without asking the driver first.

# On foot

## Harsh facts

- In 1986 21,000 child pedestrians were injured in Great Britain.
- Of these 40 per cent were aged between five and nine years.
- Of these 46 per cent were aged between 10 and 14 years.

These figures are alarming and one of the very serious things that they show is that the road safety training we give our children is simply not good enough.

## What you can do

- Teach your child the Green Cross Code.
- Enrol him in RoSPA's Tufty Club or the Streetwise Kids Scheme as soon as he is three. These are special schemes that have been devised to help parents teach their children road sense. Both produce excellent books and educational games with stickers, badges and so on to make it fun. (See Useful Addresses on page 165.)
- Teach by example.

## The Green Cross Code

- First, find a safe place to cross, then stop.
- Stand on the pavement near the kerb.
- Look all round for traffic and listen.
- If traffic is coming, let it pass. Look all round again.
- When there is no traffic near, walk straight across the road.
- Keep looking and listening for traffic while you cross.

## Using the pavement

- If there is a pavement or footpath, use it.
- Keep away from the kerb.
- Wherever possible face the traffic that is nearest to you.
- Beware of cars coming in or out of driveways — stop, look all round and listen before you walk across.
- Walk on the side furthest from traffic, whenever possible, and don't walk into the road to go round pillar boxes, lamp posts, etc.

## Clothes

Make sure your child is wearing something bright so that he can easily be seen. Navy school raincoats may hide the dirt but they are a motorist's nightmare: the fluorescent and reflective body bands that you can buy from high street chemists and most bicycle and sports shops are very effective. These will reflect the light from car headlamps and will also show up in poor daylight. Look for BS 6629. However, remember that the reflective strips are much more effective than fluorescent clothing in the dark. The strips can be seen up to 300 metres (984 ft) away, whilst fluorescent clothing can only be seen as far as 55 metres (180 ft) away.

## Safe places to play

Many accidents to children are caused because they are playing on or around the pavement. The worst culprits are balls — footballs — tennis balls — anything that can be kicked or thrown around. All too often the inevitable happens and someone misses the ball and it ends up in the road. The hard truth is that children should *never* play with

Children on skateboards are often at risk

balls near a busy road. If you have a garden use it, otherwise find a park or cul-de-sac out of harm's way.

Children on roller skates and skateboards pose similar risks. Take them to an area where pedestrians and motorists alike pose no threat, or vice versa!

If your child has to make regular journeys on his own, then the sensible thing to do is to walk those journeys with him and work out exactly where he should cross the road and when. For example, if you can't find a pedestrian crossing or some other crossing that is controlled by lights, then you will have to find a safe place on the road. Never assume it's safe to cross, even if the green man is showing. Teach your child *always* to use the Green Cross Code.

Make sure you walk the route with your child a number of times until you are absolutely sure that he can cross the road without fear

and his safety procedures are automatic. Then go through the route again and make sure he would know what to do if, for example, his normal crossing place was unusable for some reason. Finally, follow your child on the route a couple of times, perhaps walking quite a distance behind him. Tell him you are doing this so that you can make sure he is really confident. I think it is well worth doing this regularly (say once a month), just to check that no bad habits have crept in.

People often ask me at what age a child should be allowed to cross the road on his own. I don't think that there is an easy answer — it very much depends on the child, what he is used to, how good your training has been and where you live. However, in my view, no child under the age of seven should cross a road without an adult.

# On a bicycle

If you are riding a bicycle you are very vulnerable; mile for mile cyclists are about 50 times more at risk than car drivers.

It is often hard for car drivers to see people on bicycles and motorists seldom give them the

wide berth they need. When a car is overtaking a bicycle it should allow enough space between car and bicycle so that if there were an accident and the cycle fell flat it would not hit the car. Sadly this often is not the case.

## Harsh facts

- More than 27,000 bicycle-related injuries are reported to the police each year.
- One in three of these injuries occurs to a child under 15. These are just the *reported* incidents so the *actual* number of injuries is far higher.

### Choosing a bicycle

When you are buying a bicycle with your child make sure that it conforms to BS 6102. Check that:

- the height is correct so that your child is able to reach the ground while he is comfortably in the saddle
- there are no sharp edges, for example, on the mud guards
- if the bicycle has gears make sure that the gear lever is not on the crossbar as this can cause a nasty laceration, should your child catch himself on it!
- if you are thinking of buying a second-hand bicycle, check the frame very carefully and make sure there are no cracks or fractures. You should also use the check-list in the next column to make sure everything is safe before your child uses it.

### Safety check-list for bicycles

I am afraid that by the time you finish reading this book you will probably think I'm addicted to safety checks! The thing about safety is that it is not static. Although everything may be safe when you buy the article, it may well not remain so. Depending on how often your child uses his bicycle, you could check every weekend or just once a month. As soon as he is old enough, then he will be able to do the safety checks for himself, but, to begin with, you should do them together.

This is a very simple check-list that you can run through to cover the major points.

- make sure the saddle is adjusted so that it is the right height and it is securely tightened so that it won't tip back or forwards
- the top of the handlebars should be at the same height as the top of the saddle: check this and tighten the bolts securely
- it is a good idea to have a bell or a horn — make sure that it can be heard clearly at a distance
- inspect the brakes regularly and make sure that you replace any parts that are worn
- lights: even if your child is not intending to use his bicycle at night, make sure that proper

This girl is very unsafe. Keep both hands free and put your bags in a proper bicycle basket

front and rear lights are fitted to it just in case he gets stuck and is riding home in the half light. Make sure that the batteries are regularly checked so that the lights are bright. All lights at the back of the bicycle should be red and all bicycles should have rear reflectors. Make sure these are kept clean so that they can be seen properly. Many wheels have reflectors as well and these will either be amber or white
- check the tyres and pump them up if they are getting soggy
- the chain: chains often stretch; they should only have about 2 cm/5 in slack and they need to be kept well oiled
- pedals: many bicycles nowadays have reflectors on the pedals, which are an added safety feature. Make sure that pedals are kept tight and that they are not slippery. Don't buy pedals with toe caps as feet can often get caught in these. Spin the wheels to make sure they are free of wobble and make sure that the nuts are tight. Watch out for any broken or bent spokes
- if your child is carrying a

satchel, games kit, etc. on his bicycle make sure there is a proper rack or basket to hold these and that they are securely attached to it. It is vital that he has both hands free for riding and very important that the weight of his bags is evenly distributed while he is riding.

- finally, I strongly advise you to attach a safety flag to the rear of the bicycle on the offside. This will encourage other road users to give your child a wide berth.

These points will provide you with a good working guideline for a safety check but it would be sensible to ask a professional to give your child's bicycle a thorough check-up at least once a year. I know of one bicycle repair shop that has changed its name to The Bike Clinic and makes a special feature of running safety checks on a Saturday morning. That clinic deserves a lot of points for encouraging good habits — if only more would follow their example.

## Why do accidents on bicycles happen?

*Most* accidents happen because the cyclist or other road user, often a car, is not paying close enough attention to the road.

Other causes of accidents include:

- inadequate lights: many accidents happen simply because the car driver cannot see the cyclist until it is too late. Lights must be bright and the cyclist should wear fluorescent clothing and reflective strips
- loss of control: an accident can easily happen if a bicycle hits a rut or a bump or slides on some loose gravel; sometimes the child's foot can slip from the pedal either because the seat is not exactly at the right height or because he is wearing the wrong sort of shoes
- mechanical problems: I'm sure you've all felt that ghastly lurch that happens when the gear on a bicycle just doesn't engage. Check the gears regularly so that they don't slip and make sure the pedals aren't loose
- entanglement: don't let any loose clothing get caught in the wheels or in the chain — scarves especially are a hazard on bicycles so tuck them inside a coat
- cyclist's ignorance: accidents can happen simply because the cyclist doesn't know the Highway Code. Enrol your child on a proficiency course. Some councils run courses held at schools, while others have special courses in the holidays. They are usually for children of nine years and upwards. Ask for

information from the Road Safety Officer at your Council Offices or Town Hall.

Remember that, having successfully completed the course you will need to ride with your child and reinforce all that he has been taught so that he doesn't slip into any bad habits! So, make sure you find out about the course. You may find, like me, that you have to correct one or two habits of your own!

## What to wear on a bicycle

Remember that when your child is on a bicycle you want him to be very visible to other road users. Make sure that he wears *bright clothes* and *reflective tape*. His shoes should be either lace-ups or trainers — slip-ons, Wellingtons, sandals or bare-feet can be very dangerous. If your child is wearing long trousers, roll up the legs so that they won't catch in the chain or make sure that he tucks them into his socks or wears cycle clips. If you have a daughter, make sure that she doesn't wear full skirts when she is on her bicycle and avoid long coats and long scarves and any other loose clothing that could catch in the wheels or the chain. If gloves are worn, avoid the mitten-type — they must give a good grip and not restrict movement.

## When should a child cycle on his own?

There is no easy answer to this. First of all you must cycle with your child to make sure that he learns good habits and develops his road sense. If you are going to let him ride to school, he should attend a cycling proficiency course. You must ride with him at first to make absolutely sure that he is confident and certain of how to cross various roads, what to look out for and how to strap his bag securely to his bicycle. Check regularly that he hasn't slipped into any bad habits. Make sure that he learns to keep his eyes on the road ahead, to keep the ball of his foot on the pedal and that he keeps both hands on the handlebars. Try to avoid letting him ride in bad weather as road surfaces can become very slippery and it can make cycling very treacherous. Make sure that he always has enough money so that he can telephone you and ask you to come and pick him up if the weather gets really bad.

## Cyclists' helmets

At present there is no law to say that cyclists should wear helmets. However, *approximately 65 per cent of cyclists killed and seriously injured have head injuries*.

• look for BS 6863 or ANSI Z 90.4

(the American safety standard)

The safest helmets have:

- a firm 2 cm (¾ in) thick crushable inner layer (not just soft foam)
- a strong strap that won't part company from your helmet.

Bicyclists are very vulnerable — wearing a helmet makes good safety sense.

# POSTSCRIPT

I could not possibly cover all the hazards or dangerous situations in which children can find themselves in one book. However, I hope that I have highlighted some useful areas in which you can reduce the risks that your children — and yourselves — are exposed to.

It is very important to have a positive attitude to safety. This book is *not* about curtailing some of your and your children's activities. The aim has been to show you how to make these activities safer. If you reduce the element of risk, you will reduce the worry and I think you will find, as I have, you can . . .

**Play safe** *and* **have fun**

# APPENDIX

## Poisonous fungi

Agaricus xanthodermus –
  Yellow stainer
A. placomyces
Amanita muscaria – Fly agaric
A. phalloides – Death cap
A. pantherina – Panther cap
Boletus satanas
Claviceps purpurea – Ergot
Clitocybe rivulosa
C. dealbata
Gyomitra esculenta
Hebeloma crustuliniforme
Inocybe lacera
I. geophylla
I. griseo-lilacina
I. praetervisa
I. squamata
I. fastigiata
I. langei
I. patouillardii
I. jurana
I. maculata
I. napipes
I. asterospora
Lepiota cristata
L. fuscovinacea
Ramaria formosa
Rhodophyllus sinuatus
Russula emetica (when raw)
Sclerodema aurantium –
  Common earth ball
Storpharia hornemannii

## Poisonous flowering plants

It is best to assume that all parts of the following plants are unsafe
Alder buckthorn (*Frangula alnus*)
All species of buttercup (*Ranunculus*)
All spurges (Euphorbia)
Baneberry (*Actaea spicata*)
Bittersweet (*Solanum dulcamara*)

Black bryony (Tamus communis)

Black nightshade (*Solanum nigrum*)

Columbine (*Aquilegia vulgaris*)

Common buckthorn (*Rhamnus cathartica*)

Cowbane (Cicuta virosa)

Darnel rye grass (Lolium temulentum)

Deadly nightshade (*Atropa belladonna*)

Dog's mercury (*Mercurialis perennis*)

Fine-leaved water dropwort (*Oenanthe aquatica*)

Fool's parsley (*Aethusa cynapium*)

Foxglove (*Digitalis purpurea*)

Fritillary (*Fritillaria meleagris*)

Green hellebore (*Helleborus viridis*)

Hemlock (*Conium maculatum*)

Hemlock water dropwort (*Oenanthe crocata*)

Henbane (*Hyoscyamus niger*)

Hogweed (*Heracleum sphondylium*)

Ivy (*Hedera helix*)

Larkspur (*Consolida ambigua*)

Lily-of-the-valley (*Convallaria majalis*)

Meadow saffron (*Colchicum autumnale*)

Mezereon (*Daphne mezereum*)

Mistletoe (*Viscum album*)

Monkshood (*Aconitum napellus*)

Privet (*Ligustrum vulgare*)

Spindle tree (*Euonymus europeaeus*)

Spurge laurel (*Daphne leareola*)

Stinking hellebore (*Helleborus foetidus*)

Thornapple (*Datura stramonium*)

Tubular water dropwort (*Oenanthe fistulosa*)

Wild arum (*Arum maculatum*)

Winter aconite (*Eranthus hyemalis*)

White bryony (*Bryonia dioica*)

Yew (*Taxus baccata*)

*Notes:*

*Hellebore* comes from the Greek, meaning 'poisonous food'

*Aconite* comes from the Greek for 'arrow'. Extracts of these poisonous plants (*Aconitum*) were used for the tips of the arrows in ancient times

# USEFUL ADDRESSES

**British Approvals for Fire Equipment**
48A Eden Street
Kingston-upon-Thames
Surrey KTI IEE
Tel: 01-541 1950

**BBC Enterprises Ltd**
Education and Training Sales
Woodlands
80 Wood Lane
London W12 0TT
Tel: 01-743 5588

**BMA**
BMA House
Tavistock Square
London WCIN 3XX
Tel: 01-387 4499
For more information on AIDS and hepatitis B

**British Red Cross Society**
9 Grosvenor Crescent

London SW1X 7EJ
Tel: 01-235 5454

**British Standards Institution**
Enquiry Service
BSI
Linford Wood
Milton Keynes MK 146LE
Tel: 0908 221166

**British Sub Aqua Club**
16 Upper Woburn Place
London WC1H 0QW
Tel: 01-387 9302

**Brown Shipley & Co**
Rockwood House
9-17 Perrymount Road
Haywards Heath
RH16 1TA
Tel: 0444 458 144
Brokers who can provide insurance polices giving children protection after accidents, including those in playgrounds

## Caradon Mira Ltd
Cromwell Road
Cheltenham
Gloucestershire
GL52 5EP
Tel: 0242-221 221
For fail-safe valves for showers, etc.

## Child Accident Prevention Trust
28 Portland Place
London WIW 3DE
Tel: 01-636 2545
For more information and statistics

## Consumers' Association
2 Marylebone Road
London NW1 4DX
Tel: 01-486 5544
Publishers of *Which* magazine

## Fair Play for Children
137 Homerton High Street
London E9
Tel: 01-328 4973
For information about playgrounds and safety surfaces

## Families Anonymous (FA)
310 Finchley Road
London NW3 7AG
Tel: 01-278 8805
This organisation offers advice and support for families and friends of drug users

## Haemophilia Society
123 Westminster Bridge Road
London SE1 7HR
Tel: 01-928 2020

## Health Education Council
78 New Oxford Street
London WC1 1AH
Tel: 01-631 0930
Particularly useful for information about the care and treament of children, or adults, infected with HIV or hepatitis B

## Gas Alert
Cory Technology
George House
121 High Street
Henley-in-Arden
Warwickshire B95 5AU
Tel: 05642 445415
Device for detecting gas leaks

## Kidscape
82 Brook Street
London W1Y 1YG
Tel: 01-493 9845
Send a large SAE if you would like a 16-page booklet of parental guide-lines

**MASTA** (Medical Advisory Services for Travellers Abroad)
London School of Hygiene and Tropical Medicine
Keppel Street
London WC1
Tel: 01-631 4408
AIDS, hepatitis B and other infectious disease information

**National Association of Young People's Counselling and Advisory Services (NAYPCAS)**
17/23 Albion Street
Leicester
LEI 6GD
Tel: 0533 558763

**National Playing Fields Association (NPFA)**
25 Ovington Square
London SW3 1LQ
Tel: 01-584 6445

**RE-SOLV**
The Society for the Prevention of Solvent and Volatile Substance Abuse
St Mary's Chambers
19 Station Road
Stone
Staffs STI5 8JP
Tel: 0785 817885

**Royal Life Saving Society, UK**
Mountbatten House
Studley
Warwickshire B80 7NW
Tel: 052-785 3943

**Royal Society for the Prevention of Accidents (RoSPA)**
Cannon House
The Priory Queensway
Birmingham B4 6BS
Tel: 021-200 2461

**SAFA** (Safety and First Aid)
59 Hill Street
Liverpool 48 55A
Tel: 051-708 0397
For first aid kits and specialist packs to protect against HIV infection

**Safety in Playgrounds Action Group**
16 Old Hall Road
Salford
Manchester M7 0JH

**SCODA** (Standing Conference on Drug Abuse)
1-4 Hatton Place
Hatton Garden
London EC1N 8ND
Tel: 01-430 2341
For help if you suspect a member of your family or a friend has a problem with drug abuse

**St John Ambulance**
St John Ambulance Association
1 Grosvenor Crescent
London SW1X 7EF
Tel: 01-235 5231
For information on courses and for literature

**Streetwise Kids**
Freepost
Room 501 B
County Hall
London SE1 1BP
See chapter on Transport, page 151

**'Supersafe with Super Ted'** is
obtainable from
The Headpostmaster
Cardiff Head Post Office
220-228 Penarth Road
Cardiff CF1 1AA
This is a booklet for children and
includes a safety game and lots of
safety advice

**Tacade**
3rd Floor
Furness House
Trafford Road

Salford
Manchester M5 2XJ
Tel: 061-848 0351
For further information on health
and drug education

**The Terence Higgins Trust**
52-4 Gray's Inn Road
London WC1X 8JU
Tel: 01-242 1010 (Helpline)
For information about the care
and treatment of people infected
with HIV

# Telephone numbers

**Childline** 0800-1111
**Family Network** 01-226 2033
Helpline 01-242 1010
**Irish Society for the Preven-
tion of Cruelty to Children**
Dublin 0001-761293/763051
/760452
**Mothers of Abused Children**
0965-31432

**National Society for the Pre-
vention of Cruelty to
Children** 01-242 1626
**NSPCC London Communica-
tion Centre** 01-404 4447
**Royal Scottish Society for the
Prevention of Cruelty to
Children** 031-337 8539/8530

# BRITISH STANDARD NUMBERS

The British Standards Institution can help you to discriminate between good, indifferent and unreliable products. Standard specifications and requirements, written by technical experts, are produced by BSI. Companies may choose to comply with a standard or may in some cases, be obliged to by government regulations. These regulations do not apply to second-hand goods.

Standards provide tests for performance or safety, specify the dimensions of a product or any combination of these. They may also recommend the way in which goods should be used or maintained by consumers. Using standards can help manufacturers to produce goods of a consistent quality with efficiency.

If you wish to consult the standard for a product, complete sets of British Standards are kept for reference at most central public libraries throughout the UK.

When a manufacturer claims compliance with a British Standard the product may be marked BS followed by a number. The number indicates the particular standard for that product. On some goods you may also see a Kitemark or Safety Mark, as shown overleaf. This means that BSI has had samples of the product independently tested against the appropriate standard and that the standard has been complied with in every respect. Continued quality is assured through the careful monitoring of a quality system agreed between BSI and the manufacturer concerned. For advice on current Kitemark and Safety Mark licence holders for particular products

**BSI Kitemark**
This shows that the product has been made to a British Standard, and usually appears along with the relevant BS number for that particular type of product.

**BSI Safety Mark**
This shows that the product has been made to a *safety* standard. Look for it for instance on gas appliances, light fittings and power tools.

contact BSI at British Standards Institution (see page 163 for their address.)

If you have a problem with a product that does not bear a Kitemark or Safety Mark, and the retailer is not willing to help you, you can take your complaint to the Trading Standards Officer, employed by the local authority in which you bought the goods, who will be able to offer you legal advice.

Below is a list of BS numbers for items that you are likely to have already–or buy as a result of reading this book!

Baby nests BS 6595

Baby walkers BS 4648
Bicycles BS 6102
Carrycots BS 3881
Carrycot restraints BS AU 186
Child safety seats and harnesses BS 3254 (ECE reg 44)
Cots BS 1753
Domestic, mains-operated electronic equipment (TV's, microcomputers, etc.) BS 415
Domestic gas appliances BS 5386, 5258
Dummies BS 5239
Electric Blankets BS 3456
Electric fuses BS 1362
Electric plugs BS 1363
Fire blankets BS 6575
Fire extinguishers (portable) BS 5423

Fire extinguishers (aerosol) BS 6165

Fire guards:

for use with gas, electric and oil-burning heating appliances BS 1945

for use with solid fuel appliances BS 6539

for use with portable, free-standing or wall-mounted heaters BS 6778

spark guards BS 3248

Flammability of furniture BS 5852

Flammability of non-foam fillings Part I BS 5852

Flammability of foam fillings Part 2 BS 5852

Fused plugs, 13 amp BS 1363

Highchairs BS 5799

Kettles, ovens, grills, cookers, washing machines, tumble dryers, sewing machines, electric heaters BS 3456

*N.B.* BS 3456 is an important number to remember. It covers the specifications for safety of household and similar electrical appliances. This includes room heaters for use in children's nurseries and electric heaters for baby feeding bottles.

Life jackets BS 3595

Lighting sets for christmas trees BS 4647

Mattresses and pillows for cots and prams BS 1877

Nightwear (test for flammability) BS 5722

Playground equipment BS 5696

Playpens (traditional) BS 4863

Protective hats for horse riders BS 6473

Protective helmets for pedal cyclists ANSI Z90.4 or BS 6863

Prams BS 4139

Pushchairs BS 4792

Residual Current Circuit Breakers RCCBs) BS 4293

Rearward-facing restraints BS AU 202

Reflective items (strips, bands, belts, etc.) BS6629

Safety gates and barriers BS 4125

Safety glazing (glass and film) BS 6206

Safety harnesses BS 6684

Seat Belt booster cushions BS AU 185 (ECE reg 44)

Smoke detectors BS 5446

Toys BS 5665, BS 3443

# INDEX